I0622451

The Spyder's Web

Printed in the United States of America

The Spyder's Web

Is this what they call "intelligence"?

Ian Mayo-Smith

Four Pillars Media Group

Copyright ©2012 by Ian Mayo-Smith.
All rights reserved. No part of this publication may be reproduced, distributed or transmitted in any form or by any means, including photocopying, recording, or other electronic, or mechanical methods, without the prior written permission of the publisher, except in the case of brief quotations embodied in critical reviews and certain other non-commercial uses permitted by copyright law. For permission requests write to the publisher Four Pillars Media Group at P.O. Box 499, Meriden, CT 06450

This book is a work of fiction. The characters, incidents and dialog are drawn from the author's imagination and are not to be construed as real. Any resemblance to actual events or persons living or dead is purely coincidental.

Printed in the United States of America.
Printed on acid-free paper.

Library of Congress Control Number 20129448828

Cover design by Laura Augustine.

Preface

This book is a spy story. But not a very serious one. Some spy stories have been written by writers with considerable experience in intelligence work, such as Ian Fleming. The present writer can make no such claim although he did spend three years first in the Intelligence Corps during World War II and then another three years later after graduating from Cambride, so he has some smattering of knowledge of what goes on in some of the intelligence agencies. He saw a number of examples of stupidity in some of the actions taken in the name of intelligence. So this is the real reason he wrote this book. The action mostly takes place in a mythical country in South East Asia, but don't try to identify the country. The author himself could not do so.

Are any of the characters based on real people whom the writer has known? Not really. He would love to have met and worked with people like Lisa Goodbody and Rita Ryker, but unfortunately he never did. He did meet some members of MI6 (as it was then) who behaved like idiots. But this is a fantasy and a parody, not based on any reality regarding times or places or organizations.

Be thankful, if you are either British or American, that the security of your country is not in the hands of the people like those in this story.

On second thoughts maybe it would be better if it was.
Ian Mayo-Smith

Acknowledgments

The author wishes to acknowledge the help, guidance and constant encouragment he has received from his wife, Krishna Sondhi and his friends and colleagues, Brian Walsh, Maura Satchell, Catherine Wyatt-Morley and Laura Augustine. Without the wise and helpful advice of these people this book would have probably been written in half the time.

He also remembers with fondness his former colleagues in the gathering of informaion from enemies and potential enemies who were trying to keep it secret. They include all of those who worked in the Testery at Bletchley Park, and his later colleagues in Greece the late Ray Illingworth, Dennis Walker, Bill Sedgwick, Ted Annan, Peter Greenhalgh and Peter Abbott of the British army and Tom Bennetto and Ernie Keener of the US army.

There are others I cannot name without putting their lives in danger.

I thank all these former colleagues as, if I had never known them, I would not have had anything to write about.

Contents

Part 1

The Clandestine Cockney

page 1

Part 2

Enter the Stuntwoman
(and she's half Kosher too.)

page 55

Part 3

The Dominiatrix

page 97

Part 4

The Cashiered Quartermaster

page 129

Part 5

The Big Bang

page 147

Major Players in the Drama

Sid Bloggs - Maintenance superintendent in the British Consulate General in Hangkow, Hambonia

Myra Bloggs - his wife

Colonel Anthony Witherington Fairfax - retired army officer

Lady Ponsonby - status conscious lady friend of the Colonel

Lisa Goodbody - Secretary to the Consul General

Rita Ryker - Israeli Vice Consul and former stunt driver

Messrs White and Wong, lawyers in Hangkow and members of the Canadian Secret Service

Kimpoo - South East Asian secret agent

Miscellaneous consular and embassy officials, members of MOSSAD and MI6, signals intelligence technicians, and Uncle Tom Cobbley and all

Note. Some characters use different aliases at certain points in the narrative.

Part 1

The Clandestine Cockney

The Cocktail Party

"Sorry, m'dear," said Colonel Anthony Witherington-Fairfax," I know it's all rather a bore but I did not think I could ignore the Devenish's invitation. After all, the pompous old ass is Her Majesty's Consul General in this benighted spot."

"I know, dear, but did you really have to drag me along too?" replied Lady Ponsonby.

"But you know I hate going to these things alone, and after all old Devilish was your husband's best friend. I don't see how you could have avoided coming anyway."

'Yes, Bertie had a lot of strange friends but that doesn't mean that I enjoyed their company. Of course I had to go along with him as a dutiful wife."

The relationship between the Colonel and Lady P was the subject of much speculation amongst the expatriate population of the resort city of Hangkow. It was known, of course, that they were good friends and it was said that the Colonel, as a young Captain, had been best man at the wedding of young Mary Elizabeth Worthington Farthingon Squiers to the rising young diplomat Bertram Ponsonby. By resolutely refusing to offer any help whatsoever to stranded or distressed subjects of

Her Majesty, Bertam rose in his career to eventually become British Ambassador to Hambonia, the East Asian Nation in which his widow still spent most of her time. Sir Bertram, as he became, was well liked by the Hambonian authorities who felt he was a man who shared many of their deeply held traditions. When he died he was cremated and a funeral ceremony was held at which an Anglican priest, a Buddhist Abbot and a Brahmin Swami took part and laudatory obituaries appeared in both the English language and vernacular papers.

As I was starting to explain, there was speculation regarding the exact nature of the relationship between Lady P and the Colonel. Were they or weren't they? That was the nub of the question. And speaking quite frankly that had been the unanswered question even before the death of Sir Bertie. Some of the members of the Hangkow Foreign Ladies Association felt that Lady P was not quite – you know what I mean, my dear – quite as respectable as she might have been and, despite her being a titled lady, they were strongly opposed to her being the Chairwoman of their committee. It did not matter to Lady P as they were always extremely polite, even sometimes rather obsequious, to her face.

Lady Ponsonby was in her early fifties but could have passed for younger. She was slim and she had kept her figure. She had rather long black hair with no signs of grey showing, thanks mainly to various bottles she kept in her bathroom. If you had asked the Colonel, he would probably have told you that she was a "damn fine figure of a woman." She carried herself well and always managed to seem to be looking down her nose at the people she was talking to. That was perhaps the

4

only thing about her appearance that stopped her from being a very attractive woman, but it is difficult for a woman who has something like a permanent sneer on her face to appear attractive to those she considers to be her social inferiors.

The Colonel on the other hand looked like the very stereotype of the retired ex-military officers who are to be found in the mysteries of Agatha Christie and her contemporaries. He had grown rather thick around the middle and had a red face with a large moustache. He tried to speak in the same kind of aristocratic voice as Lady Ponsonby, but somehow on him it sounded rather phoney, as if he was deliberatly putting it on and not getting it quite right. That and the fact that sometimes he momentarily lapsed in a rather lower class accent made some people wonder if perhaps the Colonel was not a Sandhurst man but had come up through the ranks.

The cocktail party at the Devenishes was to celebrate Her Majesty's official birthday, so practically all the British and Commonwealth citizens resident in Hangkow were there as well as many others of the resident foreign community.

The Colonel and Lady P, sometimes together and sometimes independently, circulated among the other guests. The Colonel imbibed a good many glasses of the champagne cocktail that was being served and got rather tipsy. In fact he found it rather difficult to stand up when Timothy Devenish proposed the toast to Her Majesty.

Later Lady P had to admit that, although she had found the cocktail party exceedingly dull up until that moment, what followed was very far from boring, for clutching his stomach and making a series of most unpleasant sounds the local head of Russbank, the huge Russian banking corporation which was making steady inroads in Hambonia fell to the floor very dead.

The Sissie

The British Embassy doctor was called but it was clear that Mr Gospodinov, the unfortunate Russian banker, was very dead. It also became clear that the glass from which he had drunk the toast to Her Majesty contained poison, its taste disguised by the cheap local champagne used in the cocktail.

The Consul General soon discovered that the police in Hangkow had no desire at all to become involved in dealing with the murder. As Police Brigadier General How Rat Ran, the Hangkow police chief explained to Devenish, "You realize, don't you, Mr D that this most unfortunate murder occurred on British soil, not Hambodian soil. You see the ground and buildings of the British Consulate General are leased to the British Embassy and, therefore, just like the Embassy itself, are regarded as British territory. So you see we are not involved at all. However, we will be happy to offer you any technical assistance you require. You have only to call upon us. But personally I shall be away for the next few days. I am going on a golfing holiday in Japan, but I am sure my subordinates will be most happy to give you any assistance you need."

"I've been on to the Ambassador" Devenish later

told Colonel Witherington-Fairfax, " and he told me we'd have to deal with this affair ourselves. It is, of course, bloody awkward. I am due to attend a party at the Russian Consulate General next week and I know the CG there hates my guts. I'm rather at a loss what to do."

"But surely, old boy, you have one of the spy chaps on your staff. Couldn't you assign him the task of solving the mystery of the murder?"

"By Jove, Colonel, I do believe you've hit the nail on the head. We do have one of the MI6 chaps on staff. He is officially listed as Maintenance Superintendent. I'm afraid he is rather a common little chap, so he doesn't appear much at official functions. Went to a comprehensive school I believe, and he was born in Hackney, but I gather he is quite a wiz at languages and solving crossword puzzles and sudoku and all that sort of thing. Of course, I should assign the job to him."

"But, Tim, old man, I thought that MI6 only recruited upper class Oxbridge types, not East Enders who went to comprehensives!"

"Yes, that used to be true, but look where it got them – Burgess, MacLean, Philby and all that lot. Anyway it's not called MI6 now. It's SIS, the Special Intelligence Service. We call their agents the Sissies and the Sissie assigned to this place is named Sid Bloggs."

"Doesn't have quite the same ring to it as James Bond, does it?" said the Colonel laughing.

"No, it doesn't and Sid does not have much in common with James Bond, I assure you. But if you like I'll introduce you."

"Yes, I would like to meet the fellow."

8

Devenish went to one of the Consulate's internal phones and told a member of staff to tell the Maintenance Superintendent to come to his office.

Bloggs, if that indeed was his real name, turned out to be a man of about five foot eight, he had a face like one of those intelligent rats who learn to find their way through mazes in experiments carried out by research psychologists. He was dressed in a slightly rumpled Marks and Spencer suit and spoke with an East End of London accent.

"Mr Bloggs", said Devenish, "I'd like you to meet Colonel Witherington-Fairfax."

"'Ow d'yer-do, Colonel", said Bloggs, "O' course, I know the Colonel very well by sight. Yes, I fink I know quite a lot about the Colonel."

"Er, well," said the Colonel, "old Timmy -- that is to say the Consul General -- tells me that the problem of unraveling the mystery of this very unfortunate murder is being turned over to you."

"And, er, Bloggs," added the CG, "I have informed the Colonel what your real role in the Consulate here is."

"Yes, one of the cloak and dagger boys, eh? Just the man we need for this job."

"Well, Colonel, it's a bit outer the way of my usual work. I got a pretty good idea 'oo done it and I could easily put 'im – or 'er, of course, – outer the way, but the CG don't want any more messy deaths 'ere in the consulate. But tell me, Colonel, what is your particular interest in this affair."

It was the CG himself who answered. "Well, you see Bloggs, the Colonel is an old friend of mine. We go back a long way and I got to know him very well in India. At that time he was the Deputy Assistant Director of Military Intelligence in Jaipur. That's in India you know. So I thought with his background in intelligence he might well be able to give you a hand in this investigation."

"That's extremely thoughtful of you, C.G. What with the 'elp offered by Police Brigadier General How Rat Ran and that of the Colonel we should have this sorted out in no time at all."

The sarcasm in Bloggs's little speech went right past the C.G. and the Colonel.

"I don't think you can expect much help from the Hambodian police," said the Colonel. "I was once taken on a tour of their training academy. The Director told me 'We place a great emphasis on the use of case studies.' I asked him where they got their case studies. He then told me that the ones they were currently using were just a little bit dated. Then he pointed to a set of the complete Sherlock Holmes stories by Conan Doyle. But then he added they were well on their way to getting their whole collection of case studies updated. "It's not complete yet, but we have over fifteen volumes of Agatha Christie's Hercule Poirot cases." Then he hastened to add that they were also very keen on learning from the American approach to crime detection and he had placed an order with Amazon.com for ten Ellery Queen books."

"Yes, very amusing," responded Bloggs, "but C.G. I'd very much like to 'ave a private word wiv you if I may."

"Very well," reluctantly agreed Devenish. "Let's

go into my secretary's office. Excuse us , please, Colonel."

The moment they were out of the Colonel's hearing, Bloggs' whole demeanor seemed to change. He seemed somehow to have grown noticeably taller. He certainly stood much more erect.

"Excuse me a minute C.G." he said, and then he started a careful examination of the C.G.s desk, the pictures on the walls, the desk light and various other objects. He also took a small electronic device out of his pocket and started pointing it around the room. Finally he seemed satisfied.

"O.K." he said "your office seems clean. No bugs that I can find."

"What's going on?" asked Devenish, for Bloggs' voice now bore no trace of East London cockney, but sounded more public school and Oxbridge.

"I need to take you fully into my confidence, sir. My persona as Sid Bloggs is my cover and I would not want the Colonel to suspect that I am not what I have seemed to him to be. Also I want to ask you if you will send the Russian Consul General a polite note telling him that something has unfortunately come up which will prevent you from attending his cocktail party, but adding that you have asked the British Trade Attaché, Thaddeus Polovsky to attend in your place."

"That's all very well, but I don't know any British Trade Attaché called Polovsky."

"No, sir, that will be me. You see I want to be able to talk to my opposite number in the Russian Consulate about Gospodinov. I used to know him very well in Rio when we were both stationed there. As far as he is aware I am a Polish refugee who came to Britain as a child during the Cold War and who became a British subject and joined the SIS."

'Well, I must say you are full of surprises, Bloggs, if that really is your name."

"My name doesn't matter, sir. As long as I am at this post I am Sid Bloggs, your maintenance Superintendent."

"But why do you want to meet with this Russian spy fellow? Do you really think you can trust him?"

"No, sir, I don't trust him any more than he trusts me, but I think we can find out if we have a mutual interest in getting to the bottom of the mystery about this Gospodinov affair. From what I have been able to understand it has thrown the Russian intelligence people in this country into quite a spin."

"But you can't go to the Russian do dressed in those clothes…"

"Don't worry, sir, I will go as a highly respectable diplomat in the appropriate clobber, don't you worry. I will be leaving from my own quarters, sir, and I shall take care that none of the consulate staff see me leaving or returning."

"Very well, I'll write the note and have it sent over. But I guess I had better write it by hand and seal it myself."

"Right on, sir. It would not do for your secretary to see it."

"Tell me about this Russian spy fellow you hope to meet. What's his name?

"Well, he's calling himself Igor Karpov now and he is supposed to be the consulate archivist. But when I knew him in Rio he called himself Srecan Bozic and was supposed to be cultural attaché."

"But Bloggs, that's a Serbian name, not a Russian one, and if my memory serves me, Srecan Bozic means Happy Christmas."

Bloggs laughed., "Yes, sir, it does, but I don't think many of the good people of Rio knew that."

The Female of the Species

While her husband was having his highly confidential chat with the Consul General, Myra Levine Bloggs was surprised to receive a visit from Lady Ponsonby. That very class conscious lady had confided in the Colonel, "You know, Tony, I have been thinking about that poor little East End Jewish woman married to Bloggs, the Maintenance Superintendent. She must be awfully lonely."

"Why's that, m'dear?"

"Well, who can the poor woman mix with socially? There are no other wives in the British community who are from the working class, and besides that the woman's Jewish. I really feel it is my duty to pay her a social call."

So she went to the Bloggs' quarters and was pleasantly surprised when a good=looking young woman opened the door. She introduced herself and Myra Bloggs invited her in.

Lady P really did find Myra Bloggs full of surprises. She was a pretty woman with an oval face and brown eyes and auburn hair. She was smartly, though no doubt inexpensively, dressed. Her house was extremely neat. She spoke with an accent which, though not nearly as upper class as her own, had little of the East End cockney in it. Lady P noticed in the sitting room that Myra had a copy of the London Times open at the crossword puzzle page and that it was half filled in. There were books on the bookshelves and they were not the sort of books Lady P would have expected. There were the collected plays and verses of Noel Coward, several Bernard Shaw plays, a number of history books, Rabbi Michael Lerner's "The Left Hand of God", David Kortens's "When Corporations Rule the World" and Desmond Tutu's "God Has a Dream" as well as thrillers by Ian Rankin and John Le Carre, to name a few.

"I see you read a lot" said Lady P.

"Well, apart from the housekeeping, which doesn't take too much of my time, there's not a lot for me to do. I do belong to the gym at the Majestic Hotel and I go there about three times a week."

"Do you have many friends here?"

"Well, not among the expatriate community, but I am making friends among the Hambonians. You see, I meet them at the gym and I am trying to learn the language, but I admit it's not an easy language to learn."

"Oh, do you speak many languages?"

Myra smiled. "Not as many as my husband. He has a natural talent for languages. I speak Hebrew and Yiddish being Jewish, and I can get along in French, German and Spanish."

Lady P was impressed and said so. She herself only spoke English. She had at one time had a smattering of school girl French, but she could never really see the point of becoming fluent in another language, because, surely, all the people who really mattered learned to speak English, didn't they? Surely English was the universal language. The Americans were about the only people who could not speak it properly.

"Tell me, Myra, where did you meet your husband?"

"Oh, we met at the L.S.E."

"What's the LSE?

"The London School of Economics, part of London University."

'Oh," said Lady P, imagining Myra working as a clerk there or slaving away as a waitress in the cafeteria. "Were you working there?"

"No, I was doing my Master's degree in economics."

"Oh!"

This conversation was not turning out the way Lady P had envisaged at all. This young woman was far from being the rather downtrodden working class housewife she had imagined.

"And what was your husband doing there? Was he on the staff?"

"Not exactly, but he had been brought in to give a series of special lectures on the economics of the countries of the former Soviet union."

"Goodness me! I would never have suspected him of being an academic.."

"Well, to tell the truth the last thing he would want to be is an academic. But he does know a lot of things."

"So it would seem."

"He rather enjoys his job here. He's a natural born actor and loves playing a part. Out here he plays the part of a rather uneducated person. He says it helps him in his work."

"Oh, yes, his work. I gather from my friend Colonel Witherington-Fairfax that your husband's work is rather hush-hush."

"Yes, maybe, but I can't talk about his work. He never discusses his work with me. All I know is he is in charge of the maintenance of the Consulate General buildings and all the staff quarters."

"Of course," said Lady P., wondering to herself as to how much of that last remark from Myra Bloggs was to be believed.

Later that evening as she was having her usual glass of Harvey's Bristol cream sherry with the Colonel, she asked him, "Tony, dear, what do you make of that little man Bloggs."

"Not much," replied the Colonel. "Please don't mention it to a soul, but old Devilish revealed to me that Bloggs is actually the secret service man assigned to this consulate. I think that accent of his is fake and I don't think his real job has got anything to do with looking after the maintenance of British property here."

"Have you ever met his wife?"

"Don't think so. Bloggs doesn't come to the usual consulate parties and that sort of thing and the only time I would have seen her would be if she came with him to one of those affairs."

"Well, I went and paid her a visit this morning. And I got a bit of a shock."

"What do you mean? Was she a complete gorblimey tarted up blonde or something?"

"Far from it. She is a very presentable young woman, more so, if I may say so than some of the wives of the younger members of the consular staff. She is well educated, and it seems she has a higher degree in economics. If she were to mix with the rest at these various official consulate parties, she would stand out as head and shoulders above some of the other wives. Why do you think she hides herself away like she seems to do?"

The Colonel laughed. "Well, I can't say I blame her. If she is an intelligent and educated woman why would she want to mix with the likes of young Tony Ashton's brainless wife, or that Hambodian girl that Harry Simpson married. I imagine she was a bar girl before Harry married her."

"Yes, you have a point there," admitted Lady P, "The wives of our two Vice Consuls are not exactly people whose acquaintance a person of breeding would want to seek out. But Dick Butcher Baker the Consul and Shorty Flap-Dudel, the Counselor, both have very civilized wives, don't they?"

"Yes, I suppose so, but just now you referred to Mrs Bloggs as 'a person of breeding.' I thought she was an East End Jewess."

"Well, what if she is? She came across to me as much more a person of good breeding than either of the Ashton or Simpson women and probably better educated than the Consul's or the Counselor's wives. If you ask me there is some mystery there and I wonder what is really going on. You are close to the Devenishes, Tony, and I really think you ought to find out."

The Almond Croissant

The next day the Colonel went to see the Consul General at 10.30 a.m. He chose this time because he knew Devenish took a break and had his morning coffee at this time. He also took with him a small bag containing two almond croissants from the Italian Patisserie in the Big Q shopping mall in Hangkow, They were those horseshoe shaped things with chocolate coatings at the ends of the horseshoe and had a delicious almond flavor. Lady P had bought them and given them to the Colonel.

"I know Timid Tim loves these things," she had said, "so take these along with you when you go to beard him in his den during his coffee break. That should soften him up a good deal."

The Colonel handed the bag with the croissants in it to the C.G's busty blonde secretary, Lisa Goodbody and asked her to bring the croissants in on a plate when she brought in the C.G's morning coffee.

Although the Colonel had no appointment he spoke briefly to the secretary who then phoned the CG and he was shown in to the C.G.'s office.

"Morning, Colonel, to what do I owe the pleasure of this intrusi ….that is to say, unexpected visit?"

"Just wanted to have a confidential discussion with you, C.G., about a member of your staff and his wife."

"Oh, well, I guess we can do that over a cup of coffee." He pressed a buzzer and Liza Goodbody entered, carrying a tray with two cups, a coffee pot, glass of warm milk, a sugar caddy and three plates, on one of which lay the almond croissants."

"Oh, what's this?"

"The Colonel brought these with him, sir," answered the secretary smiling.

"Very decent of you, Colonel. You know I'm very fond of these things, but I don't often eat them. Got to watch the old waistline, what?"

"Well, to be honest, C.G. I can't really claim credit. It was really Mary - Lady Ponsonby, you know. She knew I was coming to see you and she knows that you like these things, so she got them from that Italian cake shop in the mall and gave them to me to bring along with me."

"Well. Please give her my thanks. I love that almond smell and the taste." So saying the C.G. took a bite out of his croissant. A moment late his face contorted and it seemed to the Colonel that he turned purple, he clutched at his body and fell to the floor.

"Miss Goodbody," yelled the Colonel, "come quick. Send for the doctor immediately. I think the C.G. has had a heart attack."

The secretary came in and rushed to where the C.G. sat, collapsed in his chair. She quickly examined him.

"I'll call the doctor right away "she said, "but I'm

afraid it won't do him any good. He's dead. And that was no heart attack, Colonel. You smell that almond-like smell? That's cyanide. Looks like he's been poisoned. You see, Colonel, I am not only the C.G.'s secretary I am also the resident nurse for the Consulate and at one time I used to work in the E.R. of Barts Hospital in London."

"Oh, my God," said the Colonel. "What on earth are we going to do?"

"Well, for one thing we don't touch anything. We wait for the doctor. And I think we had better call Mr Bloggs. I don't know what the C.G. has told you, Colonel. But Mr Bloggs is in charge of the security of the Consulate. I'll also call the Consul as he will have to take charge until a replacement for Mr Devenish has been named."

"Yes, of course" said the Colonel, impressed by the way Miss Goodbody had kept her cool. "You are right."

"Why don't you just wait outside in my office for the time being, sir, until Mr Bloggs and the doctor and also the Consul get here. I am sure they will want to ask you some questions.

The Colonel went through the door into the Secretary's office. Meanwhile the secretary picked up the C.G's phone and called Sid Bloggs.

"Hello, Lisa, what's up."

"I am not quite sure, Sid, but it looks like old Colonel Ditherington Fartface has just murdered the C.G. Can you come up here straight away? I'm just going to call the doctor."

"What do you mean, Lisa?"

"He seems to have given him an Italian pastry

laced with cyanide."

"Good God, I'm, on my way, Lisa," replied Sid.

"Oh, and Sid, on your way could you get hold of the Consul and ask him to come up here too? Tell him the C.G. is dead."

"Will do."

Lisa put down the phone and then sat down in the chair opposite the dead C.G. She took out her notebook and started to write down everything she could remember from the time the Colonel came in and handed her the bag of croissants. Lisa's name might be Goodbody but her real main attribute was her cool head.

Analysis

A couple of days later Sid Bloggs was at home talking with Myra as he went over the circumstances of the C.G.'s death. The post of C.G. was being temporarily filled by the Consul, Richard Butcher Baker, as acting Consul General. A communication was expected shortly from the Foreign and Commonwealth Office about a permanent replacement for Devenish, whose funeral was to be held the next day. Mrs. Devenish would be leaving very shortly thereafter.

Once again the Hambonian authorities had made it clear that they regarded the death – murder? – of the Consul General as a purely domestic British matter since the C.G. had been a British subject and the death had occurred on British soil. "Of course," the Chief of Police, had added. "It is abundantly clear that all the possible suspects in this case are British. No Hambonians are involved."

The Chief had, however, once again agreed to provide any technical help the British might require and the croissants together with the milk, coffee and sugar which had been served had all been sent to the Hambonian police forensic lab. The lab had reported that both croissants had yielded enough traces of cyanide to kill a platoon of British officials, though the coffee, milk and sugar did not appear to be contaminated.

"I am not quite sure how much we can rely on the info given us by the local forensic people," Sid told Myra, "but it's all we are likely to get."

"So the acting C.G. has dumped this whole mess in your lap has he?" asked Myra.

"Yes, he did send a signal to London asking if they could arrange for someone to be sent from Scotland Yard to help or more likely to take over the investigation, but the reply came back today. What with the Commonwealth Conference and renewed threats of terrorist activity in London, the Met was fully stretched and were unable to spare anyone to come here. So I am now in charge of dealing with both the murders."

"Typical" sighed Myra.

"Well', said Sid. "This latest murder does appear to be simpler than the earlier one. On the face of it, there can only be three suspects."

"You, mean because there were only three people who had the chance to poison the croissants."

"Exactly, first there's Lady Ponsonby."

"Yes, because it was the old biddy who bought the croissants and gave them to the Colonel to bring for the C.G.'s elevenses."

"Right, Myra. Then of course there's the Colonel himself. They were in his possession after Lady P had given them to him. And then finally there's Liza. The Colonel gave them to her and she brought them in with the coffee."

"Can you be sure, Sid that it was the C.G. and not

the Colonel who was the intended victim. There were two croissants and one was for the Colonel."

"True, Myra, but if he was the murderer he would have poisoned both because he could not know which one the C.G. would take. And he did not eat any of his. But the possibility has struck me that the Colonel and Lady P may have been in cahoots and planned this murder together."

"Yes, I know, but it would immediately have become clear that one or both of them would immediately fall under suspicion. If you ask me it would be a pretty stupid way of murdering the old buffer."

"But have you any reason to think, Myra, that the Colonel and Lady P are not stupid?"

Myra laughed. "But I am not sure they are that stupid," she said.

"Well, that only leaves Lisa. She could have poisoned the croissants when she was getting the coffee."

"I could certainly imagine Lisa having lots of good reasons for wanting to get rid of old Devilish. I understood from her that he was an impossible man to work for. She also told me once that he had made a pass at her and threatened to send very unfavorable reports on her if she did not do what he wanted. She could have seen this as a wonderful chance to get rid of him and let the Colonel and Lady P take the rap for it. But to tell the truth, Sid, I don't for a moment believe she had anything to do with it. It's not in her character, and anyway she knew enough about the old Devil to have a pretty good hold over him. No need to bump him off."

"Well where does that leave us? I checked up on the patisserie. It was never a serious thought that someone there might have poisoned the croissants in the hope of poisoning some British official, but I did go there and buy some croissants just like that ones Lady P brought. They were made the same day and they were fine. I think we can rule the patisserie out completely."

The next day a message came via the British Embassy in the capital, Pispot, to the effect that the Foreign and Colonial Office were unable to find an immediate successor to Devenish, but that after very serious consideration they had decided to ask a distinguished British citizen who was a retired senior army officer, if he would be willing to take over the post and that said retired senior officer had accepted. Colonel Witherington-Fairfax would be taking over from the next day as acting Consul General.

When he came home for lunch the next day Sid Bloggs called to Myra, "You know what they've done, love? They've made old Colonel Fartface the new C.G. It's incredible, isn't it? The Colonel is one of the most obvious suspects in this case. I think the Ambassador must have lost his marbles. Of course, Dick Butcher Baker is furious and I understand he is even thinking of resigning."

"Yes, Sid, it stinks to high Heaven," agreed Myra. "I can't blame Butcher Baker. But I wonder what the Hell the old goat, the Colonel, will do now he's in charge of the Consulate."

"God knows. Perhaps he'll make his girl friend, the old biddy who came to visit you, his deputy."

"You mean Lady Ponsonby?" Myra laughed. "Of course, she'd just love that. She'd be able to lord it over us ordinary mortals even more than she already does, wouldn't she? But I don't think he could get away with that. That's just too over the top."

"Anyway I'll get some idea of what he's planning tomorrow. He's already sent me a message he wants to meet with me tomorrow morning in his office."

The Colonel Takes Charge

The next morning Sid, in his cockney persona, presented himself at the C.G.'s office.

"Wotcher, Lisa," he said to the Secretary. "The acting C.G. said he wanted to see me."

Lisa pressed a buzzer and almost immediately the door to the inner office opened and the Colonel put his head round the door.

"Ah, good man, Bloggs. Come in will you?"

After they had both sat down the Colonel began. "I don't want you to misunderstand me, Bloggs, because I have the greatest respect for your abilities, not withstanding your lack of education and your humble origins. I am sure you are a very able fellow. But I think you will have to agree that it would be entirely inappropriate for you to continue to be in charge of the investigations into the two murders."

"Oh, Colonel," replied Sid, "and why might that be?"

"Well, for one thing not only do you not appear to have made any progress into the death of that Gospodinov fellow, but you have let another murder occur right under your nose."

"But, sir,..." began Bloggs.

"And there's another thing" interrupted the Colonel. "It is clear that someone from the Israeli embassy was to blame for murdering Gospodinov, and your wife is Jewish so it is inevitable that you would be biased."

The total injustice of the Colonel's remarks hit Sid, and he had to take a firm grip on himself not to show his anger, but he replied very calmly.

"With due respect, sir, I must point out that my wife is not an Israeli, she is British. She is a loyal subject of Her Majesty."

"But she is a Jew, isn't she?"

"Yes, sir, she is of Jewish descent, though she is not actually a practicing Jew in the religious sense."

"Makes no difference, Bloggs. In my experience all Jews, whether practicing or not, are all pro-Israeli. So I am taking you off the two murder cases."

"But sir, I must protest."

"Protest all you want, Bloggs. Put your protest in writing and I'll forward it to the embassy. However, it won't make a bit of difference. I talked to the Ambassador and told him of my decision and he agrees with it fully. From now on you are officially off the murder cases and you will get back to what ever it is you spy fellahs usually do."

"Very good, sir, I understand, but might I ask 'oo will be in charge of investigating the murders instead of me. Will you be calling in the local police to take over the investigation."

"Certainly not, Bloggs. What a ridiculous idea. They have already made it clear that they don't want to have anything to do with it and we don't want them snooping around the Consulate, do we? I am sure I can find someone who is capable of undertaking the task without being in danger of being biased by personal connections."

'"Do you mean you will hand it over to the Consul or one of the two Vice Consuls."

"No, Bloggs, they're all far too busy. I think I'll have to call on someone with the appropriate expertise but who is not currently on the consular staff."

"Oh, you mean someone like Lady Ponsonby, for example, sir?"

"I say Bloggs, that's an excellent suggestion. I would not have thought of her if you had not put the idea into my head. Thank you for that, you've been most helpful."

When Sid went home for lunch that day, he told Myra all that had transpired.

"The bloody old hypocrite. That's what he's been planning all along. It's a good thing I did not bet you that he would not put old Lady Peabrain in charge of the investigation," he said, "because I would have lost the bet."

"The old fool must be off his rocker" agreed Myra. "But I wonder why he was so concerned about me being Jewish. Do you think he could possibly have found out that before we were married I used to work for Mossad?"

"At this point I don't know what to think, love, except that he is up to no good. I am not sure how much of his pomposity and muddle headedness is just a front or how much is genuine. I am pretty sure that old Devilish did not tell him the whole truth about me and he won't find it in the personnel file kept here. I have no means of knowing what the Ambassador may have told him. But I am sure at least that he doesn't know that I have my own means of communicating with my own superiors. And I am going to have to call them on my own secure cell phone tonight."

Sid went to a locked drawer in the desk in his study and took out a green cell phone which he only used for calling on other members of the SIS network. The instrument was slightly larger than the usual present day cell phone but it contained within it a scrambler. The phone could only communicate with other similar phones which were standard issue within the SIS.

He phoned the lead SIS agent in Pispot and explained to him what had been happening.

"Hello, Root2. This is Pi R squared here."

"Roger Pi R squared, this is Root 2, receiving you loud and clear."

At this point, in fairness to the reader, it should be made clear that although they were speaking on a totally secure phone line, the SIS agents (or Sissies) never used real names. Only code names had to be used in all communications. As aficionados of the James Bond books know a code name beginning with the figures 00 denoted an agent with a license to kill, but the most senior agents all had irrational numbers as their code names. They were allowed to kill with or without a license. It will be appreciated by the perspective reader therefore that Agent Pi R Squared, known to his colleagues in Hangkow as Sid Bloggs, was a very high up Sissie indeed.

Other people in whom the SIS was interested had less exotic code names. For immediate purposes it is sufficient to explain that the code name for the Colonel, now Consul General, was "Mustard Gas"; for Lady P it was "Martianess;" for the late C G it was "Leaky Bladder"; but Myra as a former member of a (supposedly) friendly sister service, had a rather different type of Codename. She was known as "Sister 23."

However to save the reader the time and trouble of remembering all these codenames I will recount the conversation between the two Sissies as though it had been in plain English.

"It appears to be a complete cover-up and it looks as though the ambassador himself must be involved in it. On the quiet I have made a thorough search of both the Colonel's and Lady Ponsonby's houses and also of Lisa Gooodbody's apartment but could not find any trace of cyanide in any of them. I don't actually suspect Lisa anyway. It seems clear enough to me that either the Colonel or Lady P could have murdered the CG or they could have done it together, but it will be extremely difficult to pin the crime on either one of them – or for that matter on them both. And for the time being my hands are tied by the Colonel's direction that I am to have nothing to do with either this case or the Gospodinov one. And by the way I am quite convinced they are connected."

"I am sure, you're right, old boy. And I can see that I am going to have to stick my unwelcome nose into a few places here in the Embassy. Admittedly His Exceellency, the Ambassador, is an idiot but I can't even see him agreeing to the Colonel being given the CG post, unless there is something we know nothing about behind it."

"But what do you think I should do, now that I cannot carry out any investigations openly under my present cover."

"Well, old man, I think we are going to have to move Sid Bloggs to the Embassy in Tokyo. But a Trade Delegation is coming to look into ways British Airways can cooperate with Hambonia to help the development of the tourist industry here. Among the delegation will be a former RAF Group Captain, Roddy O'Bhuzagh. By the way how is your Belfast accent?"

"Not as good as my Cork accent, but I expecct it will probably be good enough to fool most people. But what about Myra?"

"Well. Myra is quite used to changing personalities, isn't she? Could she pass for German?"

"Yes, easily, she talks German like a Berliner."

"Excellent. Well, you get ready to wrap things up at the Consulate. Meanwhile I'll get a complete set of new documents ready for the two of you and let's meet in Bangkok a week from today."

The Trade Delegation

There was some surprise at the Consulate General when it was announced that Sid Bloggs was leaving, having been posted to the British Embassy in Tokyo. The new C.G. seemed rather relieved even though he had been informed that the post of Maintenance Superintendent would for the time being remain unfilled and that other members of the staff would have to take over the maintenance duties.

"Well, my dear", said Lady P to him. "He was such an unsuitable man after all. Such a dreadful accent. I can't think what that nice little woman, his wife, saw in him. She was far better educated than he was. I imagine her people were much better class than his."

"Yes, I know, and I didn't like the way he always seemed to be snooping around, looking into things that didn't concern him. That old fool Devilish should never have let him head up the murder investigation."

"Don't speak ill of the dead, dear. It might give people the wrong idea."

"Between you and me I'll say what I like about him. The truth is the truth whether some other people like it for not."

The one person who really seemed sorry that the Bloggs were leaving was Lisa Goodbody.

"I am really going to miss you and Myra" she had told Sid. "They are mostly such a lot of stuffed shirts around the Consulate. The two of you are the only two staff members whose company I can enjoy."

"Don't worry too much, Lisa. I think you might meet some interesting new people quite soon," replied Sid.

"What do you mean, Sid?"

"You'll see."

A week later the British community in Hangkow learned of the arrival of the British Trade Delegation. It was headed by a fairly senior politician and was to be accommodated in the Hard Knocks Grand Hotel on the sea front in Hangkow.

The head of the Delegation, Sir Humphrey Bummfree, called upon the C.G. and asked him if he could assist the delegation by providing some secretarial assistance to one of their key members, Group Captain O'Bhuzagh. When Sir Humphrey made it abundantly clear to the C.G. that said C.G. might very soon lose his post if he did not comply, the Colonel reluctantly agreed that his own secretary, Miss Goodbody could be seconded to the delegation for as long as her services were required.

Lisa was rather pleased when she learned about this arrangement. She could not stand the Colonel and was delighted to be getting away from him for some time. She was invited to a cocktail party being given by Sir Humphrey who treated her with respect and told her how delighted he was that she would be working with them.

"But most of the time you will be working directly with Group Captain Roderick O'Bhuzagh. I'd like to introduce you to him now. Come with me. That's him over there."

He led Lisa over to a very upright man with a large handlebar moustache.

"Oh, Roddy, I'd like you to meet Miss Goodbody, who's been loaned to us by the Consul General."

"Delighted to meet you, Miss Goodbody," said the Group Captain in a broad Ulster brogue. "And I'd like you to meet my wife, Brigitte."

Something about the petite woman introduced as the Group Captain's wife struck Lisa as vaguely familiar, though she could not quite place what it was.

"Well, I hope you'll excuse me. I have to mingle with our other guests," said Sir Humphrey, and he was off.

"Vy don't vee move to zat table over zere in zat corner" suggested Brigitte.

So the three of them moved to a table in the corner of the room that was pretty much out of hearing of the rest of the guests. Then in the unmistakable voice of Sid Bloggs the Group Captain leaned over to Lisa and said "Well, Lisa, me ole love, 'ow are yer. It's good to see yer again."

"Oh, my God" exclaimed Lisa, and spilled the daiquiri she was holding onto to the floor.

"Well," said the man now known as Roddy O'Bhuzagh. "I did say that you might meet some new friends soon."

An Alliance is Formed

The next day Lisa went to meet with the Group Captain.

"Lisa, I am sure you have realized by now that there is something very fishy going on at the Consultate and that old Colonel Fartface is mixed up in it up to his whiskers. I am pretty sure that he murdered the former C.G. and that he was involved in the death of Gospodinov. I think it more than likely that Lady Ponsonby is working in cahoots with the Colonel but I am not absolutely certain about that."

"Yes, Sid – oh, by the way what do I call you now. I can't go on calling you Sid, can I?"

"No, when we meet formally, just call me Sir. But informally call me Roddy. That is how I am known to the rest of the Delegation. Only Sir Humphrey has any idea of the real reason I am here."

"So I suppose you are here to investigate what is really going on at the Consulate."

"Exactly. It was plain for all to see, Lisa, how anxious the Colonel was to get me off the investigation into the Consul General's death. There was nothing much I could do while playing the role of the maintenance superintendent, so my people arranged to move me out and bring me back here in this disguise."

"Yes, Sid – I mean Roddy – but why does Myra have to speak with that funny accent."

Sid laughed. "Well, if you look into the file which has been supplied to the Consulate, you will see that I served as Air Attache in the British Embassy in Berlin for some time and while there I met and married a German girl named Brigitte Steinmetz."

"I take it that Myra – or should I say Brigitte? – is fully aware of what is going on."

"Oh yes, Lisa. She is fully in the picture. You see she has secret service experience of her own. I met her when SIS was working with Mossad to uncover an Arab Muslim extremist group that was planning to blow up the Houses of Parliament. She was a member of Mossad."

"Good Lord, Sid! Oh, dear, I am going to have some difficulty remembering to call you Roddy and to call Myra Brigitte. But I was going to say that I am not sure you did us British a favor by stopping the terrorists from blowing up Parliament!"

Sid/Roddy laughed. "I know how you feel, Lisa. When you see what those clowns have done to the country. I sometimes feel the same way myself. By the way I call my wife Gitta for short. Brigitte is a bit of a mouthful. So you just call her Gitta when we are meeting informally."

"Oh, I'll try to remember all this. But, by the way, what is your real name? Is it Sid or something quite different."

"Never mind my real name, Lisa. I have almost

forgotten it myself. But my wife's name really is Myra. We saw no reason to change it previously. But for this assignment she has to take on a whole new personality."

"Don't you find it difficult, keeping on changing your personalities?"

"I am used to it, Lisa. I am still the same old bloke underneath, you know."

"Yes, but which bloke is that?" asked Lisa.

"The one that values you as a friend, Lisa. You always got on well with Sid Bloggs, didn't you?"

"Yes, I did. I liked you as Sid."

"Well, apart from the accent, Lisa, that was mostly the real me. And the real me has always liked you and trusted you. And that was why I asked my bosses to arrange for you to work with me on this new assignment."

At that moment, Myra, alias Brigitte, came into the room.

"That goes for both of us, Lisa. There's no one we'd rather have working with us than you."

"Thank you , Myra. I am feeling quite choked up." The two women embraced.

"But please try to remember to call me Gitta, that's all. We cannot risk having our identities found out. You may find it easier once I start talking all the time with my German accent. It is quite phony but it is good enough to fool most people."

"OK. But what exactly is it that you want me to do, Sid – I mean Roddy. This is going to take a bit of getting used to."

"Lisa, I want you to be my eyes and ears inside

the consulate. You can come and go easily between here and the consulate and no one will ask any questions. But the first thing I want you to do is to find out every single thing you can about the Colonel and Her Ladyship. I am quite sure that we will find something about him that is not quite kosher."

"OK. I'll do my best."

"I know you will, Lisa. They say that military intelligence is the lowest form of intelligence, but I needed someone really intelligent to help me on this case and I have realized that you are one of the most intelligent people on the consular staff, even though some of the senior people don't seem to realize it."

"Thank you. Yes, I know I am brighter than most of that bunch. But please don't patronize me."

"Sorry, Lisa, I did not mean to, and what I said was sincere."

"Well, I know that both of you are very bright people yourselves. So I have to assume that you have had me very thoroughly checked out before confiding in me and taking me on as your assistant."

"Too right, Lisa. Of course, I did. I already trusted you and we both felt you would be the best person on the consulate staff to work with us. But I would have been in very serious trouble, if I had taken you on without an in-depth security check."

"OK, so you must know about my family. My Dad's a retired Chief Superintendent in the Special Branch. My older brother Fred, is a Detective Chief Inspector in the Met. My younger sister Kate works in G.C.H.Q." (Government Communications Headquarters, the agency that monitors all types of communications including those in codes and ciphers.)

"Oh, yes, I know all that, Lisa, and I knew you were a registered nurse, but you haven't mentioned that you yourself were a Detective Sergeant and that before you joined the consulate staff here, you had already applied to join MI5, the old domesstic security service. But I can't think why they turned you down."

"What makes you think they did?" asked Lisa with a smile."

Investigating the Colonel

Lisa took full advantage of her ability to move freely without let or hindrance between the temporary offices of the Trade Delegation and her regular office in the Consulate General. Since she had full security clearance she was able to get hold of the personal files of any member of the consulate staff without questions being asked. She was careful to avoid going to her regular office in the consulate at times when she knew the Colonel would be in the C.G's office. During the period of her secondment to the Trade Delegation the Colonel's secretarial work was being done by a local Hambonian member of the consulate's clerical staff.

She also stayed out of the way of Lady Ponsonby as far as she was able, but she was able to talk to other members of the consulate staff about the actions (if any) that Her Ladyship was taking to solve the mystery of the two murders. It did not seem that Her Ladyship had made either much progress or much effort.

A few days after her earlier meeting with Roddy and Myra/Gitta, she handed Roddy a written report. The salient points were that the Colonel's earlier life seemed shrouded in mystery. None of the documents to which she had had access indicated what the

Colonel's regiment had been, though there had been a mention of his having spent time attached to the Arab Legion when he was a young officer. To Lisa it looked as though someone, probably the Colonel himself, had recently been through his personal file and had removed most of the documents that the SIS might have been interested in.

There was not much information in the file of Lady Ponsonby. She was not and had never been a full time employee of the consulate and to Lisa the arrangement by which she had been put in charge of the investation into Devenish's death appeared most irregular. However, the actual letter from the Ambassador approving her temporary appointment as a "temporary Assistant to Her Majesty's Consul General, charged with carrying out an investigation into the death of the Consul General" appeared to be genuine enough.

Lisa decided to phone her friend Happy Golukky who worked as one of the staff in the Ambassador's office. Happy told her that the Ambassador had not thought the appointment a matter of any great importance.

` "It was too bad the old boy committed suicide in front of guests," she said, "so H.E. just wanted to tidy up the details. You know, to find out if there was anything in the work of the consulate that was preying on his mind, or anything like that."

"Where the hell did you get the idea that he had committed suicide?" asked Lisa.

"Well, that was what the Colonel reported. He told H.E. that he thought that the Devenishs were having marital difficulties and that the old boy had become so depressed that he couldn't take it any more and took

43

poison."

"My God, Happy, that's a total distortion of the facts. Devenish was poisoned by someone who gave him an almond croissant laced with cyanide."

"Heavens, Lisa, that's not what we've been told."

"What's more what you've been told came from the Colonel and it was the Colonel who gave Devenish the poisoned croissant."

"Are you certain of all this, Lisa?"

"I was standing right there when it happened."

"Good God!"

"Now listen, Happy, for God's sake don't let anyone else know about this conversation. The fact is that the C.G's death is being investigated here. The Colonel tried to shut down the investigation but it is still going on. I can't tell you any more. Please, please, don't say anything to anyone in Pispot until you hear something official."

"O.K., Lisa, my lips are sealed, but how the hell have they managed to keep the truth from our people here? Sounds like the Colonel himself would be the number one suspect, and he's the one who phoned H.E. to give him the news."

"I'll try to call you on a secure line later, Happy, but meanwhile don't say a word."

Lisa lost no time in reporting this conversation to Roddy, who did not seem unduly surprised.

"I have been on to my people in Pispot" he told Lisa, "so I had already heard about the false version of events that the Colonel had given. He is pretty brazen in the way he tells his lies. And I am not surprised either about the missing pages in his file. I didn't expect you to find out much about Lady P."

"I am going to have to ask our friends in London to make some enquiries for us. I am by no means certain that the Colonel has not reinvented his identity at some time, and I very much doubt that Lady P is exactly what she claims to be."

So Roddy got on to his green cell phone and had a long conversation with colleagues in London. He also had a conversation with his wife and suggested she might help by using the contacts she still had with former colleagues in Mossad.

Within a short time he learnt that the War Office in London had no records of a Colonel Anthony Witherington Fairfax. But a photograph of the Colonel, taken by Myra without the Colonel's knowledge, had been emailed to London and members of SIS had circulated it privately among senior or retired members of the military. Eventually a retired Warrant Officer from the Royal Army Service Corps, was found, who said that, though he couldn't be quite sure, the photo reminded him of a former colleague.

"But he weren't no Colonel, I tell you. 'E was an RQMS, a Regimental Quarter Master Sergeant, that is. And 'is name weren't anything fancy like Witherington-Fairfax. He was plain Tony Fairfax, that's what."

Follow-up enquiries had been able to trace the career of the former RQMS. He had in fact been commissioned as a QM officer with the initial rank of Lieutenant. He had served in India and had risen to the rank of Captain (QM). Roddy explained to Myra and Lisa that in the British army one way for a ranker to rise up to and through commissioned rank was being promoted to a commissioned Quarter Master post.

"But I am afraid his career as a British army officer ended there" Roddy told them. "He was cashiered –
that is dishonorably discharged owing to the discovery
of serious discrepancies in the stores. Reading between
the lines I think he had been selling off British army
weapons and ammunition to the leaders of rebel tribal
groups in India, but it does not sound as if they were
able to prove it. They could only prove that the supplies
were missing."

"So he got off relatively lightly?" said Myra.

"Yes, it seems so."

"Were you able to find out what happened to him
after that?" asked Myra.

"Yes, it seems he entered the service of an Arab
sheikh in one of those small emirates in the Middle East.
He promoted himself in rank and gave himself a fancier
sounding name, because the next record of him showed
him calling himself Lieutenant Colonel Witherington
Fairfax and serving in the Arab Legion. He retired
some years ago and has been calling himself Colonel, a
title to which he may or may not have some legitimate
claim."

"But he is a crook, anyway," said Lisa.

"Oh, yes," agreed Roddy, "he's as crooked as
they come, but he's by no means as stupid as he looks;
that pose as the pompous blundering old buffer is just
an act."

"Yes, and he's been getting away with it for quite
some time," said Lisa.

"Well as a Group Captain I am of exactly equal
rank to that of a full Colonel in the army, so I think I am

going to have a little social chat with the Colonel as one retired senior officer in HM's armed forces to another, and I'll see if I can learn anything more about him."

"O.K. so now we know quite a bit more about the Colonel than we did, but what about Lady Ponsonby?" asked Lisa.

Her Ladyship's Background

"You may be surprised about what we've learned about Lady P," replied Myra. "I talked to a friend of mine in the Israeli Consulate and asked her if she knew anything about Lady P. She laughed and said 'You're probably too young to remember her, Myra, but did you ever hear of the musical hall artiste Little Lizzie Squires?'

"The penny dropped and I realized why all along Lady P reminded me of someone. It also explained why she took the trouble to pay me a visit when she did. I think she just wanted to make sure whether I recognized her or not."

"Oh, please, do explain," said Lisa excitedly.

"Well, when I was about ten or eleven there was a very popular music hall singer and dancer, who, like me, was from the East End. She went under the name of Little Lizzie Squires. She was quite talented and she was very ambitious. But she wasn't quite good enough to make it to the very top in the theatrical profession. So she left the music halls, which were dying out anyway, and she began working in upscale clubs, where she felt she could meet people who could help her move up in the world. There she met a young diplomat named Bert Ponsonby. He was quite dazzled by Little Lizzie and fell for her head over heels. They got married. He rose in the diplomatic service and was eventually knighted. And that explains how the woman I had seen on the stage as Little Lizzie Squires – by the way she later changed the spelling of her surname from Squires to Squiers – I suppose she thought it sounded more upper class - and so she became Lady Ponsonby. I understand she was born Mary Elizabeth Squires but along the way she added in those additional names so that by the time she married Bert Ponsonby she had become Mary Elizabeth Worthington Farthington Squiers, but I don't think you'd find any mention of Worthington or Farthington on her birth certificate."

"Oh," said Lisa, "so I suppose all that stuff about her being aristocratic is a load of crap. She doesn't really come from the upper class anymore than you or I do."

"No," replied Myra, "it's all an act, but she had always been a fairly good actress."

"How long is it since her husband died?" asked Lisa.

"About four years, I believe."

"And did he die a natural death?"

"I see you have a suspicious mind" commented Roddy.

"Well, yes, she's always seemed to be so close to the Colonel. It makes me wonder."

"Well, the answer to your question is 'possibly.' There were one or two rather strange things about the way Sir Bertram died. He had seemed to be extremely fit right up to the time of his death and he was only in his late fifties. Officially he died of a heart attack, but there were suspicions that that heart attack might somehow have been induced."

"But, do you think she did him in somehow?"

"I have an open mind, Lisa," replied Roddy. "It is not impossible,but I don't really have any particular reason to think she did."

"Anyway we do know that she's not what she makes herself out to be, don't we?"

"Yes, Lisa, in a way that's true but I don't think she has been telling any outright lies. She never talks about her background, and she was legally married to Sir Bertram and she's quite entitled to call herself Lady Ponsonby."

"All the same," said Lisa, "it makes you wonder."

White and Wong

It had been a quiet day in the law offices of White and Wong. Normally they were kept pretty busy since they were the only lawyers in Hangkow who were qualified and able to practice in both the British and the Hambonian courts.

Mr White was a Jamaican of African descent and was extremely dark skinned. Mr Wong was a white European looking man. His great grandfather had been Chinese from HongKong but had married an English woman and all their male descendants had also married English women, so that Mr Wong's Chinese ancestry was hardly perceptible except in one respect and that was his inability to pronounce the letter R. It always come out as a W. By a curious coincidence Mr White also suffered from this same speech defect although in other respects his accent was pure Oxbridge.

In criminal and civil cases Mr White always acted for clients he believed to be in the right, i.e. innocent in criminal cases. He once told a friend "It would be wong to do otherwise." But Mr Wong often defended clients who he strongly suspected were guilty. As he said

"Every accused person has a white to a good defence."

Although they were partners and close friends they often argued between themselves over the "whites" and "wongs" of numerous issues.

They were both sitting talking in their chambers drinking their morning lattes when their Secretary, Miss Hoo Dun Itt, buzzed them to let them know that Group Captain Roddy O'Bhuzagh had come to see them without an appointment.

"Well, show him in," said Mr Wong.

Roddy came in and shook hands with both lawyers and apologized for coming without first making an appointment.

"That's quite all white", replied Mr Wong.

"What I have come about is highly confidential and I would be most grateful if you would not say anything to anyone else about my visit to you."

"Don't wowwy about that," said Mr White. "You know as lawyers it is always wong for us to discuss our clients' affairs."

"Yes, of course," said Roddy. "Now I believe you were the legal representatives of both the late Sir Bertram Ponsonby and the more recently deceased Mr Devenish."

"Yes, that's quite white" said Mr Wong. I dealt with Sir Bertwam, and my partner dealt with Devenish."

"Well, I am engaged in a highly confidential investigation and I need to know the main provisions of the wills of these two men."

"Of course" said Mr White, "if you had asked us that while the two men were still alive we could not have given you the information. That would have been completely wong and would have got us into sewious twouble. But, since they are both dead, the wills have become public information, and we can let you have copies if you like."

"That would be great. And I really appreciate it."

"Fine, why don't you just have a cup of latte with us and wait, and we will get Miss Hoo to make copies of the two wills."

"Thank you very much."

While they drank their lattes, the three men talked about cricket, particularly about the current test match between England and the West Indies, until Mr Wong abruptly changed the subject.

"I suppose you have also talked to Goldstein and Steingold," he asked.

"No, why should we have done that?"

"Well, they were the people who wepresented the Iswaeli Embassy in the case that was bwought against Lady Ponsonby under Iswaeli law. I understand that Her Ladyship managed to settle with them out of court and the case never came to us."

"I did not know that an Israeli law firm had offices here."

"Well, technically they don't, but there is a Vice Consul at the Iswaeli Consulate Genewal who seems to wepwesent them."

At that moment Miss Hoo came back with the copies of the two wills and handed them to the Group Captain who thanked her for them.

"Well, Mr. White, Mr. Wong, you have been extremely helpful and I thank you very much indeed."

"No twouble," said Mr. Wong.

"No, no pwoblem at all," added Mr White.

"Oh, said Roddy in the best Lieutenant Columbo fashion as he was just going out of the door, "Just one more thing. Could you give me the name of the Israeli Vice Consul who represents Goldstein and Steingold here?"

"Of course," said Mr Wong. "His name is Emmanuel Emmanuel."

"Just ask for Manny Manny at the Iswaeli Consulate; that's what everyone calls him", added Mr White.

"Thanks very much. I'll be off to see him right away."

Part 2

Enter the
Stuntwoman

(and she's half

Kosher too)

Rita Ryker, the Mystery Biker

When Roddy paid a visit to the Israeli Consul in the hope of seeing Manny Manny he was told that the former Vice Consul had been recalled to Israel.

"Well, has anyone taken over the work that he was doing here?'

"Of course they have. Perhaps you would care to speak to Miss Ryker, the new Vice Consul."

"Indeed I would."

"Unfortunately she just went out on her motor bike a short while ago. Why don't you phone and make an appointment to see her."

"Thank you very much. I will do that."

Just as Roddy walked out of the Consulate door and was making for his car, he heard the roar of the engine of a very powerful motorbike. It was being ridden by an attractive leatherclad woman in her late thirties. She removed her crash helmet to reveal a mane of curly black hair. Remembering what the man at the Consulate had told him, Roddy approached her.

"Excuse me, but are you Miss Ryker, Vice Consul here."

"Yes," she said smiling and putting out her hand,

"that's me. I'm Rita Ryker. And who are you?'

"My name's Roddy O'Bhuzagh. I am with a Trade Mission at the British Consulate General."

"Now isn't that interesting. I only got here a few days ago and I never quite expected to meet an Irishman working for the British Consul General. Anyway I think we've met before, haven't we? Only you weren't called Roddy O'Bhuzagh then. You're Myra's husband, aren't you. I was a guest at your wedding."

"Oh, my God," exclaimed Roddy. "I didn't recognize you. You're Rita Ryker, the Mystery Biker, aren't you? I should have recognized you as soon as I heard your surname and the mention of a motor bike. But this is a bit of a change for you isn't it?"

"Yes, well, I was getting a bit tired of doing all the stunt driving and my circus act. There was too much traveling and I wanted to settle down. But tell me how's Myra? And why are you calling yourself by that ridiculous phony Irish name?"

"It's a long story, Rita, but why don't you come round and have dinner with us tonight. Myra would be delighted to see you."

"I'd love to, and then we can really talk."

Roddy gave Rita the address of the apartment where he and Myra were staying, and added, "We'll see you at seven."

When Rita arrived that evening, Myra opened the door. "I can't believe it!" she said and the two of them went into a hug that lasted several minutes.

Roddy brought them all drinks and the conversation flowed. Rita and Myra had been best friends at school. It had probably been a case of opposites attracting each other, as Myra had been the serious student, who had gone on to get a first class honors degree at the London School of Economics, while Rita had excelled at sports. At the age of 18 she had literally run away to join a circus, becoming a trick cyclist, then moving on to motorbikes. She had eventually joined Fred Fleetwood's Stunt Drivers Show, which appeared at state fairs around the US. She had also done stunt driving for movies both in the US and the UK. Meanwhile Myra had been recruited by Mossad. While working for Mossad she had met and married Roddy. But the two women had stayed in touch with each other for some years, until their frequent changes of address and Myra's equally frequent changes of aliases had caused them to lose touch.

"Eventually," explained Rita, "I realized that I could not go on doing the same thing for ever. The constant moving around was getting to be a strain and really gave me little chance of having a stable relationship with anyone. My biological clock was running, and so I decided to do something about it. I started by doing correspondence courses and managed to get a degree. Then I started reading for the bar in England and managed to eat the requisite number of dinners and pass the bar exams. So I became an attorney, but I found the life of a young woman barrister in England was not so easy, so I went to Israel and qualified as a lawyer there. Having a Jewish mother I was automatically given Israeli citizenship, so I joined the Israeli Diplomatic Service."

"That's quite a story, Rita," said Roddy.

"But what about you two? When I met you at your wedding, you were very vague about your job and you didn't call yourself Roddy then, did you?"

Roddy and Myra laughed. "No, " replied Myra, "he had to use his real name for the wedding. He was actually born as Jack MacKay, and that is still his legal name, and mine of course is Myra MacKay, though for most purposes I continued to use my maiden name as Myra Levine. But this job has made it necessary for him to use a whole number of different aliases. And when he has to use a new surname I have to use it too, but I usually do not change my first name, although he does. So for the time being my name is Brigitte, or Gitta for short. I am German and I talk viz a German accent." She put on a thick German accent as she spoke the last few words.

"I assume from what you've been telling me that Jack works for the secret service."

"Yes, Rita," admitted Myra's husband, "I am a member of the Special Intelligence Service, the SIS, but please Rita, keep that under your hat."

"Don't you find it a bit confusing having all these different names – or rather aliases? And what should I call you?"

"When we're outside, please call me Roddy. But when we're alone, just the three of us, you can call me Jack. But you might find it easier if you just stick to the one name, Roddy, at least until I have finished this assignment. It's less confusing that way."

"I've got used to it now, Rita," added Myra, "At first I got really mad at having to keep changing what I called him. But now I've got used to it. Mind you he hasn't been Roddy long. Until just recently he was Sid Bloggs, complete with cockney accent."

"Good Lord, it must make you feel giddy! But tell

me what is the reason for all this?"

"Yes, dear, I think you had better come clean with Rita, don't you?"

"Yes, I think I must. I can rely on your to keep what we are going to tell you as strictly confidential, can't I?"

"I guess so," said Rita.

Sid Bloggs/Roddy O'Bhuzagh/ Jack Mackay then told Rita about the whole situation he was investigating, the two murders; their doubts about the Colonel; the origins and current position of Lady Ponsonby and how she fitted into the case; the Colonel's anxiousness to get rid of Sid Bloggs; how the new character of Roddy O'Bhuzagh had been brought in so that he could continue to investigate the murders and find out what was really behind them. He also described how he had found an ally in Liza Goodbody, the Colonel's secretary.

When he had finished, Rita asked "Don't the Colonel or Lady Ponsonby have any suspicions that you are the same person as Sid Bloggs then?"

"No, I honestly don't think they have," said Roddy.

"Well, it's priceless, isn't it? Fancy Little Lizzie Squires turning up in Hambonia as a titled lady. I can remember my Dad taking me to see her in some show in the theater. But you know, Rita," added Myra, "I think Jack really missed his vocation. He should have been an actor. He manages to change his whole personality."

"And it's not going to be easy for me to remember to call you Roddy and Gitta." said Rita "But it's been great to see you both again,and it's been quite revealing to hear what you've both been up to. But I still don't know why you came to see me at the Consulate this morning, Roddy."

Roddy's Angels

The next evening Lisa, Rita, Myra/Gitta and Roddy met in Myra and Roddy's apartments. Lisa was the last to arrive and as she came in she took one look around the room, and said "Hey, three women and one man, does that remind anyone of something?"

No one came out with an answer, so Lisa said, "Think back to old TV series."

"Oh, my God," burst out Rita, "you mean Charlie's Angels! I guess we must be Roddy's angels."

"But there is a bit of a difference," argued Roddy. "In that series you never saw Charlie. You only heard his voice. He himself was never around. So although you three are indeed all angelic, I am no Charlie."

"I don't know about that," said Myra in a stage whisper. "Sometimes I think he's a proper Charlie."

"I'll let that typical wifely remark pass" said Roddy.

"It's all right, dear," responded Myra. "We're not going to be Charlie's angels. We'll be Roddy's angels. But as we all now know your real name is not Roddy, any more than it is Charlie."

"O.K. but remember for all purposes my name is Roddy now."

"Yes, and remember to call me Gitta," added Myar, "but I suppose when you hear me speaking with my phony German accent, that will remind you."

"Fine," said Liza. "And it's a pleasure to meet you Rita, but I still don't know why you asked us here, Roddy, and how exactly does Rita fit in."

Roddy spent the next twenty minutes bringing Rita and Liza fully up-to-date on his investigations.

"O.K. I understand all that you've told us," said Rita after Roddy had finished, "but there are two things I do not understand. One, exactly why were you coming to see me at the Israeli Consulate General yesterday, and two, if the SIS already knows that the Colonel is a crook and an impostor, why is he being allowed to continue in the position of Consul General here?"

"The answer to your first question is that I wanted to find out more about the law suit involving Lady Ponsonby and the firm of Goldstein and Stein-gold who, I am told, were being represented by your predecessor at the consulate. Anything you can find out about that would be very helpful."

"O.K. I'll see what I can find out. But what about my second question?"

"That's a bit more difficult to answer. We – that is to say my SIS colleagues and I – have reason to believe that behind the two murders there is something much more sinister in which the Colonel and probably Lady P are involved. We think it involves possibly illegal shipments of arms to Al Quaeda. If we were to take any action against the Colonel now it might put the whole of the larger operation in jeopardy."

"Oh, I see," said Rita, "and I am a bit surprised that you have been able to take Liza and me so fully into your confidence."

Roddy smiled, "Don't worry, Rita, I got full clearance from London before doing so. I am free to take you both and also Myra fully into my confidence on this assignment. But I also have to warn you that there is a good deal of danger attached. I am fairly well convinced that the Colonel is in fact a remorseless killer and that more than likely Lady P is his accomplice. If either of them suspected you of involvement in this investigation – I don't know what they might do. For one thing, if you have to go to any official cocktail parties or anything like that be very careful about what you eat or drink."

"In what way do you think the Israeli consulate might be involved?" asked Rita.

"I don't know exactly, but I learnt from Karpov, my opposite number at the Russian consulate that Gospodinov, the man who was murdered at the Devenish's place, had been involved in some legal arms sales from Russia to the Israeli government. Then somewhere along the line the arms involved had been diverted. They never reached Israel and there was a strong suspicion that they had ended up with Al Quaeda. Gospodinov was investigating this. The Israelis were, not unnaturally refusing to pay for the arms they had never received. Gospodinov's investigations had somehow or other caused him to come out here to Hangkow, though exactly what the connection was is not clear. Karpov was either unable or unwilling to fill me in on that subject. Then there is the curious business of the lawsuit involving Lady P and the Israeli law firm, which was being handled by your predecessor. Until we know what that was about we don't know whether it is relevant to the other business or not."

Myra interruped, "Add to the mix two other facts. I believe that both the Colonel and Lady P are strongly anti-Semitic."

"That doesn't surprise me," said Liza, "but what makes you so sure?"

"I went to the British Council library here and I know the librarian well. I got her to tell me what books the Colonel and Lady P have taken out from the library. I was shocked but not surprised when I saw the list. The Colonel apparently does not read much but nearly all the books that either of them had taken out of the library had a strong anti-Jewish slant."

"You never mentioned this before, Myra" said a surprised looking Roddy.

"Well, it didn't seem important, but it does seem relevant now."

"You said there was a second thing" said Liza.

"Yes, the second thing is that the Colonel served with the Arab legion and spent a lot of time in the middle east. He may well have become a sympathizer with the Arab cause and, given his anti-semitism, he may well have became an extremist, an Al Quaeda sympathizer."

"Admittedly, that's speculation," agreed Rita, "but you could be right."

"Well, Roddy, what are our next moves?" asked Lisa.

At the Israeli Consulate

When Rita returned to the Israeli consulate the next day she tried to find out exactly what Manny Manny, her predecessor as Vice Consul, had done in his capacity as representative of the law firm of Goldstein and Steingold, but her search of the files, in what had been his office, revealed nothing. She also asked around among her colleagues at the consulate, but again she got nowhere. Even her secretary, Rachel Stern, who had of course been Manny's secretary, could not tell her anything.

"I'm sorry, Miss Ryker, I know he was doing something for the firm, but it must have been very hush hush as I never saw any of the papers. He handled it entirely himself."

"Isn't that rather odd?"

"Yes, I thought it was extremely odd. But that was just like Mr Emmanuel. He was a lone wolf kind of guy. To tell you the truth" she added in conspiratorial tones, "I think he was Mossad." Then she paused thoughtfully for a moment, wondering if she had said too much. "Oh, dear" she said. "Are you Mossad too, Miss Ryker, or shouldn't I ask that?"

Rita laughed. She had, of course, checked out the confidential files of Rachel Stern, and found Rachel had a very high level of security clearance.

"No, Rachel, " she admitted, "I am not, but if I was I would not mind you knowing it since you are going to be my secretary and by the way, do call me Rita."

"O.K. Miss Ryker, I mean Rita. But can I ask you a question? I heard that you were British and that you had been a circus performer. Is any of that true?"

Again Rita laughed.. "So the tongues have been wagging already have they? I don't advertise my background, but it is no secret really. Why don't we go and have lunch together in some quiet place and I can tell you all about my background and you can fill me in on yours. I hope we are going to be friends as well as colleagues."

"Oh, yes, Rita, that would be great."

Later that afternoon Rita got through to her colleagues at the Israeli embassy in the capital, Pispot, and tried to find out what they knew about Manny having represented Lady Ponsonby in the law case, but her colleagues there either did not know or would not tell. She put a call though to Roddy's office and when Lisa picked up the phone she said to her.

"I have been trying to find out more about the case in which her ladyship was involved and in which my predecessor represented the law firm she dealt with, but I have not been able to discover anything about it."

The next morning she was summoned to the Consul's office. He did not look pleased.

"Miss Ryker," he said, "I hope you will concentrate on the work you are being assigned here and that you will not waste your own and other people's time on matters that do not concern you."

"Of course, Sir."

"It has been reported to me that you spent a lot of time yesterday making enquiries about your predecessor's involvement with the law firm of Goldstein and Steingold. May I ask what business this was of yours?"

"I was merely trying to be helpful to a member of a friendly agency, Sir. I understand that a British subject was involved and the British authorities asked me for my assistance. I was not aware that I was treading on corns, sir."

"Don't try to be funny, Miss Ryker. You have interfered in a sensitive matter. I need to know the name and position of this member of the 'British authorities' who called you."

"I am sorry, Sir. He had one of those funny British accents and I did not get his name."

"Then how in hell were you going to phone him back?"

"I wasn't going to phone him back, Sir." lied Rita. "He said he would call again later to see if I had any information for him."

"I am not sure whether I can believe you, Miss Ryker, but if and when he does ring back you are to have the call switched immediately to me. Understood? And I would remind you Miss Ryker that this is your first appointment in the diplomatic service and that you are on probation for your first two years of service."

"Yes, Sir."

When Rita returned to her own office, Rachel was waiting there, anxious to know why Rita had been summoned. She saw Rita was seething with anger.

"Oh, dear," she said. "You look as if the old shlang has been putting you through the ringer. I'm afraid he is not a good bloke to work for. Nobody here likes him."

Rita told Rachel what had happened, adding at the end "I probably shouldn't be telling you all this, but he really made me mad."

"Well, I'll tell you what I think," said Rachel. "I think you've stumbled into some very hush hush Mossad business."

Later that day Rita got on her bike and was going to meet Roddy, Myra and Lisa at the local Starbucks, when she happened to pass the car which Lady P was driving.

When she got to the Starbucks she rushed breathlessly in and addressing Myra she burst out,

"My… I mean Gitta, you'll never guess who I have just seen."

"Keep your voice down, Rita," said Myra in her Gitta voice. "Ve don't vant anyone listening to our conversation. But tell me, who did you see?"

"I'll swear it was Little Lizzie Squires. You know, a lot older than when she was on the stage, but I am sure it was her. She was in a British Consulate car and she looked very stuck up. I wonder what she's doing here."

Myra laughed. "We're all wondering that, Rita. She's now known as Lady Ponsonby. Apparently she married some Brit diplomat who got himself knighted and also got himself killed or at least he died rather mysteriously."

"You mean she bumped him off?" blurted Rita.

"Vell, that's not an impossibility" admitted Myra.

"Look," said Roddy. "before we take this any further I think we should move to our apartment. This is too public a place."

"O.K." agreed Rita, "I'll meet you there in five minutes, but before we go, just give a thought to this. The Israeli Consulate keeps a list of all Jews resident in this dump, but Lizzy Squires is not on the list and I am sure there is no Lady Ponsonby on it either."

"I can't say I'm surprised" said Myra, You and I know she's Jewish, but I suspect she has been denying it for years."

"Well," said Rita, "I know I'm only half kosher, as my Dad was a goy, but I've never disguised the fact that my Mum was Jewish. In the East End we all knew Lizzie Squires was a genuine 100% Jew and her grand-dad was a Rabbi."

"Actually, Rita, you've raised a very important point," said Roddy, "but let's talk about it in our apartment."

Lady P as Murder Suspect

When they resumed their conversation, back in Roddy and Myra's apartment, Roddy first brought Rita completely up to date with all their investigations and ideas.

"But what you were telling us in Starbucks puts a new perspective on things. We strongly suspect that the Colonel has links with Muslim extremists but if Lady P is a Jew, albeit a closet Jew, she is hardly likely to be in sympathy with the Colonel. The Colonel, on the other hand is most unlikely to suspect Lady P of being a Jew or a Jewish sympathizer.

"My guess is that Gospodinov was investigating what had happened to the Russian arms destined for Israel but which disappeared. Now suppose he had got on to the Colonel's trail. The Colonel would then have a strong motive for killing him, but there would be no reason for Lady P to be involved in any way with the murder.

"The Colonel on the other hand would have every reason to take me off the investigation into the murder. So he turns to his friend Lady P, whom he trusts and gives her the job but basically tells her not to look too hard for a solution.

"We are all agreed, I think, that Lady P is no fool, so she immediately realizes what the Colonel has been up to, but goes along with the idea that she will do as he wants. But then she goes and gets hold of some poisoned patisseries one of which kills the Consul General. But what if her real target was the Colonel?

"My God, Roddy, you seem to be suggesting Lady P might be a Mossad agent" said Rita, looking startled.

"Why not?" replied Roddy, she'd make a perfect undercover agent. Who would normally suspect her?"

"Well, if she was, and if Mossad was involved in the whole business, it would explain why the Consul gave me such a hard time yesterday when I was making a few inquiries," said Rita.

"Well, if you are right we are dealing with not one but two ruthless killers. It's scary," said Lisa.

"There's just one objection that I can see," said Myra, "I don't think a well trained Mossad undercover agent would make a mistake and kill the wrong man. I am wondering if Devenish had begun to have suspicions about the Colonel and that someone tipped the Colonel off, so the Colonel poisoned him. That would make the Colonel guilty of both murders."

"But why would Lady P go along with him?"

"I don't know, but anyway the idea that Lady P is a possible Mossad agent and definitely pro-Israel, is all based on supposition. She denied being Jewish. Perhaps she sympathizes with the other side."

"On the other hand," said Myra, "maybe that's all part of her deep cover. It might also explain why she came to visit me. She could well have known that I was a former Mossad agent, and she wanted to check me out."

"I think" said Roddy "that I had better pay another visit to Messrs White and Wong, and see if I can find out any more about this mysterious law firm Goldstein and Steingold."

Back to White and Wong

"How nice to see you again, Group Captain," said a smiling Mr White as Roddy was shown into his office the next day. "How can I help you?"

"Well, you and your partner were very helpful when I came to see you last time I was here. I was hoping you might be able to help me again with a another piece of information."

"I am always happy to help a fellow RAF officer."

"Oh, I did not know that you had been in the RAF, Mr White."

Roddy felt a little nervous. He did not want to blow his cover. His briefing, as he was given his new identity, had perforce been rather brief, and although he had served his country in many different roles he had never been in the Royal Air Force and, unlike James Bond, had never flown an aircraft.

"Oh, yes, I was in command of a squadron made up entirely of people with roots in the Caribbean. We called ourselves The Wild Winged West Indians."

"Were you, by Jove,"

'Yes, but I never aspired to the exalted rank of

Group Captain. I was a mere Squadron Leader."

(Editor's note.)

1. For the benefit of any ignorant person who might be reading this chronicle, it should be explained that the rank of Group Captain is the equivalent in the Royal Air Force to a Colonel, with eagles on his shoulders in the U.S. Air Force, whereas a Squadron Leader is equal to a major. Thus Roddy's (phony)rank was two steps higher than that of Mr White.

2. For the convenience of the reader (and also the typist of the manuscript), the speech of Mr White and Mr Wong will for the rest of this tale be reported as though they spoke normal English and did not replace all their Rs with Ws.)

"Does your colleague also have a military back ground" asked Roddy.

"Yes, he does but he is rather reticent about it. You see, he came up through the ranks. He won the Conspicuous Gallantry Medal as a Sergeant helicopter pilot, was commissioned in the field and rose to be a half Colonel. He also won the Military Cross. It really was a very distinguished record."

"I'll say it was," agreed Roddy. "But I would never have suspected it,"

"No, and please don't mention it to him. Sometimes, if I want to rile him, I call him Colonel and he gets quite mad at me."

` "How strange."

"Yes, it is, isn't it. But as I said he is a very modest man. But tell me what did you want to see me about?"

"Last time I was here you mentioned an Israeli law firm that was involved in some dealing with Lady Ponsonby. Their name was Goldstein and Steingold. Apparently they were represented here by a Vice Consul, named Emmanuel Emmanuel. That in itself seemed rather strange." While Roddy was speaking Mr Wong had quietly entered the room.

"Anyway," continued Roddy, "I went to see Mr Emmanuel and was told that he had left. He has apparently been posted somewhere else. But I did manage to meet his replacement, a Miss Ryker, whom I happened to have known socially in England. She wasn't able to tell me anything, but she promised to make inquiries. But later she told me she was severely taken to task by the consul for having tried to do so. Seems to me that something rather fishy is going on."

At this point Mr Wong interrupted. "It's all right, White, he said. "I have just got clearance. We can level with the so-called Group Captain."

Roddy was taken aback by Wong's remarks, but he saw that both White and Wong were smiling at him in a friendly fashion.

"It's OK ," said White. "We know who you really are, but you obviously have not been briefed about us. We both work for CSI."

"You mean Crime Scene Investigation?" asked Roddy incredulously.

"No" replied White, laughing. "I mean Canadian Special Intelligence."

"Good Heavens" gasped Roddy "I would never have guessed, and I thought I had been well briefed about all the other intelligence agencies here in Hambonia."

"Well, we have been quietly here as sleepers" replied White, "and I think most people have forgotten about us, including, I sometimes think, our own HQs. But to be serious for a moment, we have for some time been interested in both the Colonel and Lady P. Our position here as the only lawyers qualified to act both in the U.K. and Hambonia gives us a great advantage – and by the way our legal qualifications are quite genuine."

"Unlike your rank as an RAF Group Captain" added Wong with a smile.

"Anyway" went on White. "It did seem to us that the time had come for us to share with you what we know, and we have just got the authority from our HQ to do so. And the first thing we can tell you is that there is really no such law firm in Israel as Goldstein and Steingold."

"Or at least if there is, they have never had any dealings with Lady P," added Wong.

"The second thing is that Mr Emmanuel, or Manny Manny as he was known, is a member of Mossad, and not only that, he is a member of Mossad's elite Death Squad. In other words one of their expert and specialized assassins."

"Well," said Roddy, "I was beginning to suspect something of the sort. But do you think it was he, who killed Gospodinov?"

"Well," commented Wong, "that's problematical. If Gospodinov had been screwing the Israelis over the arms deal, they could have had a reason to get rid of him, but there doesn't seem to be any reason to suspect that and besides I don't think for one minute they would have bumped him off in a way that might have put suspicion on them. They need this connection with the Russian arms suppliers and Gospodinov was that connection. But there is one thing that seems to me to be perfectly clear."

"Oh, what's that?"

"It is that Lady Ponsonby is without doubt a covert agent of Mossad."

"So it is extremely unlikely that she was in any way responsible for that murder?"

"Then that would leave Colonel Fairfax as the most likely candidate."

"It would seem so."

"Well, this is getting more and more interesting," said Roddy, "but there is one more thing that puzzles me. If Emmanuel was a Mossad agent and, as you have said, a member of the Death Squad, why have they not replaced him with another Mossad agent?'

"Oh, you are quite sure that Miss Ryker is not Mossad.?"

"I would stake my life on it," said Roddy.

"In that case do you think her secretary could be? She's a girl called Rachel something, I believe."

"I really don't know," answered Roddy, "but I can find out what Miss Ryker herself thinks."

"You know her well enough and trust her enough to ask her that?"

"Yes, I do" replied Roddy firmly. "She is an old and very good friend of my wife and I trust my wife implicitly on such matters."

"Yes, and of course, your wife is herself a former Mossad agent," said Mr White.

"Well, gentlemen, it is obvious that you have really been doing your home work. But tell me one thing. What have you been able to find out about Colonel Fairfax?"

It turned out that White and Wong had uncovered almost exactly the same information that Roddy had done..

Finally it was time for him to leave and go back to his apartment. As he was leaving Mr Wong looked at him with a grin and said, "Now you had better get on to your own people to check us out and find out if we really are what we say we are, Group Captain."

Big Scare at the Israeli Consulate

Naturally the first thing Roddy did as soon as he got the chance was to get on his green cell phone to his colleagues in the SIS to check up on Wong and White's story. It did indeed check out.

"Why was I not told all this earlier?"

"Well, the Canucks only gave us the information yesterday. It does seem to bear out what Wong and White said about their own HQ seeming to have almost forgotten about them."

Later he passed on what he had learned to the three "angels", Myra, Lisa, and Rita, but that day they did not get as far as deciding on their next moves. However, the next morning Myra got a call from Rita at the Israeli consulate.

"If you want a really good laugh," she said, "I think you should think of some reason for coming over here to the consulate."

"Why? What's up?"

"You'll see, if you just come here."

When she got to the consulate, Myra found the security much tighter than usual, She had to produce her Israeli passport before they would allow her in.

(Myra had dual citizenship, British and Israeli.) She had to drop her phony German accent and go into the consulate under her real name, not as Brigitte O'Bhuzagh. She passed a number of armed military personnel before she got to Rita's office.

"Why all the tightened security and all the soldiers all over the place?" she asked Rita.

"Well," said Rita you know why we have such a large building for a small consulate here?"

"Sure," replied Rita, "it's because of IDIOT/HAT."

"You mean the Israeli Defence Institute for Overseas Training, slash Hambonian Army Training?"

"That's right. There's a group of about thirty Israeli army men here. I think half a dozen of them are officers under the command of a full Colonel and the rest are senior non-commissioned instructors – you know, sergeants and the like. They are training the local units of the Hambonian army."

"Yes, I am familiar with that."

"Well. You probably also know that it is only a small part of this building, the front part on the first two floors, that is actually used for the normal consular work. After all, Israel does not have major commercial interests here, and there are not too many Israeli citizens living here or coming here as tourists. The rest of the building is given over completely to IDIOT. Off the record the rest of us usually refer to them as the Idiots, just as you refer to your SIS people as the Sissies."

Both women laughed.

"Well, the basement of this building is where the army transport is garaged. Then the rest of the ground and first floors are where the NCOs quarters are. Then on the second floor they have their administrative offices, and finally on the third floor there are quarters for those of the officers who do not have apartments in the town and also the officer's mess."

"I wasn't aware of that."

"Well, they employ an elderly Hambonian as nightwatchman in the basement. His job is just to make sure that no one can break in and try to steal or sabotage the vehicles. Mind you this building is very secure and the nightwatchman is hardly necessary in reality."

"But there is also a penthouse on the top of the building, isn't there? You can see it from the ground. What goes on there?"

Myra laughed and added, "As if I didn't know!"

"Yes, of course," agreed Rita. "It's supposed to be very hush-hush but I guess everybody in the consulate knows about it. It's the place where the Mossad people occasionally house Hambonians who are working as agents for them. The buzz is that at the moment there is a man suspected of being a double agent who is in reality working for one of the Arab countries. I heard he is being held there against his will and being interrogated by the Mossad people here."

"Yes," said Rita. "I know what Mossad interrogations can be like. The man must be feeling pretty desperate if he really is a double agent."

"Well, let me tell you about what happened last night. Captain Levinson and Lieutenant Perlman, the two army officers living on the third floor were woken up about 3 a.m. by a terrible noise which seemed to be coming from one of the lower floors. They could hear screaming and also a lot of banging noise. They both got out of bed and came out of their respective rooms in pajamas and dressing gowns and they met in the corridor. The both had automatic weapons with them. So they crept down the stairs to the second floor but the noise appeared to be coming from below, so they kept on going down until they were in the basement. They talked to each other in whispers. In the end they concluded that one of two things might has happened. Possibly someone had got into the basement and was trying to steal one of the vehicles and had been intercepted by the night watchman, resulting in a violent confrontation. The other possibility that struck them was that the desperate spy in the penthouse had somehow escaped and was trying to make his way out of the building when he had been apprehended by either the night-watchman or one of the soldiers on the ground floor, again resulting in a violent confrontation. Eventually the two officers identified the noise as coming from behind a door in the basement. So they stood either side of the door with their guns at the ready and at a nod from the Captain they kicked open the door. And what do you think they found?"

"I've no idea."

Rita could hardly hold back her giggling laughter as she went on with her story.

"What they found was a very scared wizened little old Hambonian man, who practically pissed his pants when he saw the two guns pointing at him."

"You mean it was the night watchman?"

"Yes, it seems he had brought a couple of bottles of Snakehead beer with him, when he came on duty. That of course was quite against the rules, but nobody bothered much about the little night watchman. He drank both bottles and after some time he began to feel the need to relieve himself. So he went into the toilet in the basement but somehow or other he got himself locked in and he could not get out. So he started shouting, trying to get one of the soldiers on the floor above to come and get the door open, so he could get out. But they apparently did not hear him so he started screaming and banging on the door from the inside and it was that noise that woke the two officers on the third floor."

"How come the soldiers on the ground and first floors did not hear him. The noise must have been pretty loud if it could wake the officers on the third floor."

"That is indeed the question, Myra. And it is the reason for all the tightened security this morning. The Colonel in charge of IDIOT is raging with fury and the Consul is extremely angry too. They are both currently holding a meeting with all the IDIOT personnel. They are very concerned about the security breach that allowed the night watchman to bring in two bottles of beer undetected. And they also want to know why none of the men on the ground and first floors was woken by the noise,"

"Yes, Rita, I can see why they would be concerned about the old man bringing in two bottles of beer, because, if he could do that, he could equally easily have brought in a bomb. But I guess the explanation as to why the men slept through all the noise was that there had all been drinking. Had they in fact all been out celebrating or something?"

"You've hit it, Myra. Apparently Warrant Officer Bloom, one of the idiots, got engaged a few days ago and he gave a big bash for all his mates to celebrate it. They had all had a lot to drink."

"Well, that explains everything, doesn't it?"

"Yes, it does, but that doesn't quite explain all the fuss and palaver that is going on this morning. I think there must be something else behind it as well, but I've no idea what it is."

Back to White and Wong Once More.

Myra, of course, repeated all that Rita had told her to Roddy.

"Of course, I can understand the consulate staff and the army people being very concerned about what happened, though I must say the idea of the two army officers going downstairs with automatic weapons at the ready only to find the disturbance was caused by the night watchman who had locked himself in the loo - Well, it is very funny. I mean funny Haha . But the reaction of the Consul and the Colonel seems to have been out of all proportion to the incident. And that seems funny too and this time I mean funny peculiar."

"Yes, you're right, Myra. I think I might pay a trip to our old friends Messrs White and Wong to see if they can throw any light on this."

When he got to the lawyers' offices he discovered that they had heard all about the incident at the Israeli consulate.

"I should think that by now almost the entire expatriate population of Hangkow knows all about it, " commented Wong. "The Isarelis have for the time being anyway become the laughing stock of Hangkow."

"But as far as I can gather the Israeli consulate seems to be in a state of near panic. Certainly they are overreacting to a fairly simple matter. There must be more to what happened than what we know."

"You're quite right, Group Captain – by the way, shall I continue to address you as Group Captain, when I know that you have never been in the RAF."

"Well, of course, there's no need to do so in private, though it would help if you would continue to do so in public. I really don't want my cover to be blown."

"Yes, we understand perfectly, don't we White."

"Of course we do, Wong."

"Well, as I was saying" continued Wong, You are quite right. They do have a much more serious matter to concern them."

"Let me make one guess," said Roddy. "In all the kerfuffle last night, the man they suspected of being a double agent escaped."

"How very astute of you, Roddy, Mind if I call you Roddy."

"Not at all said Roddy. But as I am sure you already know that is not my real name."

"Ah," said Mr Wong, sighing. "What after all is a name? A rose by any other name would smell as sweet. And an MI6 agent is an MI6 agent by what ever name he or she may go."

"How right you are," responded Roddy. "But do you have confirmation that this spy escaped."

"Well," said Mr White. "We do have certain sources within the Israeli consulate that we can rely on, just as I am sure that your friend Ms Ryker will be able to confirm this for you in due course."

"I must say, I am very impressed with the extent of your range of sources of information," said Roddy.

"We have been here a rather long time, and it has enabled us to get well established and we have steadily enlarged our network of informants."

"It would certainly seem so. Anyway, I thank you gentlemen for the information."

"It's nothing. You would have soon found out for yourself anyway."

"Yes, I suppose I would. But thank you anyway."

As soon as Roddy had left their office, White opened one of the doors leaving out of the back of the room where they had been talking to Roddy. He spoke in Hambonian and said "You can come out now, Kimpoo. The English spy has gone." and a small Hambonian, rather thin and pale came into the room, His days in the penthouse of the Israeli consulate, being constantly questioned during the night as well as the day, and being given very little to eat, had taken its toll on him. He was looking forward to the first decent meal he had had for some time. Among Mr White's unsuspected accomplishments was that he was an excellent chef.

....

Later that evening Roddy met with his three "angels" and told them what had transpired at White and Wong's.

"Do you think they were being straight with you?" asked Myra.

"I don't think they were lying., but I am not at all sure they told me all they know."

"But it does seem that they are involved more

deeply that we would have suspected, doesn't it," suggested Lisa.

"I think you're right, Lisa, but I have no idea in what way they are involved. But tell me, Rita, have you seen anyting happening at the Israeli consulate that might suggest their involvement."

"Not really, Roddy, but I'll keep a look out, especially since they have told you they have a source there."

Roddy leaned back in his chair and thought for a moment, then he turned to Lisa and said "I don't think we have enough office space, do you, Lisa?"

Lisa looked puzzled. "I haven't noticed that we didn't have enough space, Roddy. What makes you bring that up?"

"It's not so much the size, it is the convenience, Lisa. In my work – and I am speaking about my job in the Trade Delegation – I often need to have a suitable place to interview important Hambonian business men and government officials, and the poky little office we have been given is not suitable."

"Yes, of course, Roddy," said Lisa catching on quickly. "You're absolutely right. Tell me what did you have in mind?"

"Well, I happened to notice, when I went to see White and Wong, that there is an office suite right next to theirs which is vacant and is up for lease. I am sure it would suit us very well. If we could lease that, we could move there. It would be much more convenient for us and it would also relieve some of the pressure on the other members of the Trade Delegation. I am sure Sir Humphrey would be only too delighted to get rid of us."

"Sounds an excellent idea, "agreed Lisa. "Do you want me to prepare a memo for Sir Humphrey?"

"Yes, Lisa, please do. I'll have a word with him. I know he'll back me up, and as a matter of fact, since we won't need the whole suite, we could even let some of the other members of the Trade Delegation have a room or two. But I will personally select the rooms that you and I will occupy. We will almost certainly need to make some minor modifications to the building."

"Oh, what sort of modifications?'

"You'll see. Okay, we'll start on that tomorrow, but meanwhile we should give some thought about the said Consul General, the good – or rather not so good – Colonel Fairfax. What's the betting he was somehow mixed up in the escape of the spy in the penthouse of the Israeli consulate building?"

"That's an interesting thought," said Myra. "Do you think the spy in the penthouse was in some way involved in the business of the Russian weapons going astray and the murder of Gospodinov. If so he might be acting for some Arab power, and we have good reason to believe that the Colonel has connections with Arab terrorist organizations."

"Yes, Myra, my mind has been working along those lines, but there are a lot of 'ifs'. We need to get some definite evidence."

The New Offices

The next day things went very quickly. Lisa wrote
the memo which Roddy signed and sent to the Consul
General through Sir Humphrey Bummfree, who as
Head of the Trade Delegation, gave it his full backing.
The deal was done with the owner of the building in
record time. It is not certain whether that was because
the real estate broker used by the British officials had
some hold over the owner or whether the British paid
well over the market rate for the lease, but within two
days Roddy and Lisa moved in. Roddy made a phone
call to his colleagues in the capital, Pispot and a couple
of technicians employed by MI8, the wireless intelligence branch of the British intelligence service arrived
with equipment to make the minor modifications which
Roddy had mentioned to Lisa.

Roddy took two rooms which were immediately
adjacent to the offices of White and Wong, in fact they
shared a dividing wall with the two lawyers. First
Roddy had the walls of their rooms made absolutely
sound proof, then he had the technicians made a hole in
the wall about 6 inches by 6 inches and deep enough
that it just didn't go right through the wall into the

lawyers' offices. In this hole the technicians installed a wireless device. After that they covered the hole with a light covering. It would have taken an expert to see that there was anything unusual about the wall. Then they put a receiver and recording device on Roddy's desk. They followed exactly the same procedure in Lisa's office. From now on Roddy and Lisa were going to be able to listen in to any conversation, phone calls, etc. that took place in White and Wong's offices as long as their receivers were turned on. The work done by the technicians was done at night so that any noise they might make while doing the installation would not be heard by White and Wong.

When the work was done and all the furniture for their offices had been delivered two other members of the Trade Delegation, not involved in any intelligence duties moved into the rooms not required by Roddy and Lisa.

"Well," said Roddy, after the move was completed. "I think I will just go and pay a purely social call on our Canadian friends and let them know that we are their new neighbors. Why don't you come with me? It will be interesting to see their reactions."

So the two of them went in to the lawyers' office. Both men were present when they went in and looked mildly surprised to see them.

Roddy explained that they had just moved into the office suite next door to theirs and introduced Lisa as his colleague, Major Lisa Goodbody. Mr White offered them coffee and after a brief period of small talk, they left and went back to their new offices.

"Well, they didn't seem exactly overjoyed to find

that we were moving in next to them, did they?" said Lisa, "But why did you introduce me as 'Major' Good-body."

Roddy laughed. "Well, they know all about me. They know I'm, SIS and I've never served in the RAF, but they don't know all about you and now they'll be trying to figure out exactly what and who you are."

A little later Roddy and Lisa turned on their receivers. They heard a whispered conversation between Mr White and Mr Wong. White was saying, "What do you think this is all about, Wong. Do you think they moved in next door so that they could spy on us?"

"I don't know what to think, White. I thought we had played along very well with the so-called Group Captain. In fact we have been very open except for one thing."

"You mean about Kimpoo."

"Of course. And there's no need for them to know about him, is there?"

"By now he must know about Kimpoo's escape from the Israeli consulate building, but if anything, I expect he suspects Colonel F of being behind that."

"Yes, that would be the obvious thing for him to think."

"In fact I wonder how the Colonel is reacting to the latest events. I don't think he has a clue about the Group Captain and his team and what they're up to."

"No, I don't think he does. The Colonel is cunning, but I don't think he's very clever."

"Yes, I think that sums him up very well. And the Israeli agent seems to have him completely under her spell. He doesn't seem to have a clue about what she is really up to."

"You mean the former Lizzie Squires."

"Yes. You know I saw her performing once at a theater in Manchester. I was sent by the RCAF to do a course with the RAF. That was a long time ago, about twelve years ago I should think. But, you know, she was damn good. I really thought she would become a major star like Vera Lynn or Gracie Fields but she never made it to the top."

"I wonder how many people in the British colony here in Hangkow realize that the Lady Ponsonby, who gives herself such airs here, is the cockney girl who was quite a success in variety shows in Britain."

"Not too many I should guess, but any members who used to live in the Jewish community in the East end of London would probably have recognized her in spite of her efforts to give herself a more aristocratic persona."

"Yes, I keep forgetting that she's Jewish."

"Dammit, man, she's a covert Mossad agent."

At that moment as they were listening in to this conversation Roddy and Lisa heard a noise that sounded like a door opening and closing. Then they heard an unknown voice speaking in the Hambonian language and one of the two lawyers, they could not be sure whether it was White or Wong replying to him in the same tongue. They did hear the lawyer address the newcomer as Kimpoo.

Roddy gestured to Lisa to turn on her recorder.

"I'm going to have to send this to Pispot to one of my colleagues there to translate it for us."

"Mmm. This is getting interesting, Roddy, isn't it?"

"Very interesting, Lisa. The sooner we know what our Canadian friends are up to the better. It sounds as though the mysterious Mr Kimpoo has been working for them under cover for quite some time."

Part 3

The Dominatrix

Where is the Colonel?

The next morning when Roddy got to the office, he found Liza already there in a very excited state.

"Roddy," she said, "I think one of us should go to the British Consulate General. As I was coming here I saw some of the other girls. They had been called in for an urgent emergency meeting. I don't know what's up but it seems like it might be something important."

"OK, Lisa, I suggest you go there and try to find out what's happening. Although you've been seconded to work with me, you are still a member of the consulate staff and you have more reason to be there than I have. Besides that I don't want to be there more than I have to in case the Colonel or someone starts to rumble who I really am."

While Lisa was gone Roddy got on his green cell phone and called his colleagues in Pispot to find out if they had managed to get the recording of White and Wong's conversation with Kimpoo translated.

His colleague, Bertie Watt-Knott told him, "We've not finished it yet, but we have got quite a lot, though it does not seem to make much sense. One of the lawyers, I think it is White, asks Kimpoo if everything is ready down below and Kimpoo goes into a lot of details. He says something about a bench and secure fastening on the floor. He asks when the guests will be arriving and says he has got enough food in to last several days if they need it. Finally he asks what he should do with the fat one when they are finished with it. Of course, this is not an exact translation. Some Hambonian words could be translated quite a number of different ways, but you can probably get the general drift from what I have told you. We'll send you a full translation after we have finished going through the recording."

Roddy thanked Bertie and sat down to try to figure out what Kimpoo's conversation in the office next door was really all about. He was at a loss.

About an hour later Lisa returned.

"Roddy, they are in a terrible tizz at the consulate. It seems Colonel Fairfax has gone missing. He usually gets there very early. His driver goes to fetch him from his house at 7 a.m. on the dot. But this morning he went there as usual and waited outside, as he usually does, expecting the Colonel to come out. But this morning the Colonel did not appear, so he went and rang the bell, but he got no answer. He tried several times and he tried banging on the door and making a lot of noise, but still nothing happened. Then he went round the outside of the house looking in all the windows, but he saw no sign of life. In the end he came back to the consulate and told the consul that the consul general seemed to be missing. The consul got on the phone to all the places where he thought the colonel might be including the hospital and the police station, but he got nowhere. He just seems to have disappeared. I say, Roddy, do you think he's done a bunk."

"Yes, that's possible but I rather doubt it, Lisa. Do you have any particular reason to suspect he might have done so?"

"Well, yes, I do. First there is the fact that we suspect him of being up to no good and of interfering with the supply of Russian arms to the Israelis. He might have realized that we are on to him. But that's not the main reason I think he may just have buggered off."

"What's the other reason, Lisa."

"Well, Roddy, it's Lady P. No one has seen her and it looks like they may have run off together."

"Hmm, that's really interesting Lisa, but given the fact that it seems he's working for Arab terrorist organizations and she is a covert Mossad agent, it seems unlikely they would run off together."

"Yes, but Roddy, everyone thinks of them as a couple and you never know what anyone might do when people fall in love, and you know Roddy, that does happen even with old people like the Colonel and Lady P."

"Is that what people in the consulate are thinking?"

"Yes, Roddy, I think that's what most of them are thinking."

"Well. We'll see. But I am not convinced. Can you come round to our apartment this evening? I want to discuss this with Myra and Rita too."

Roddy Theorizes

By the time Roddy met with the three angels in his and Myra's apartment, no further information had came from Pispot.

He brought Myra and Rita up-to-date on the day's events. He asked them how they would interpret them and was not surprised that they all felt that the theory that Lisa had earlier mentioned, i.e. that the Colonel and Lady P must have run off together had to be the right one.

"OK, " he said, "We'll accept that as one possible explanation but I have been thinking – relying on the little grey calls as Poirot would say."

"Oh, dear, I hope you didn't strain yourself, Roddy'" said Myra.

"Thank you, my love, I appreciate your wifely concern, but I think I have survived my mental efforts unscathed."

"Oh, good, I am so relieved, you had really got me worried."

"OK, you two clowns," interrupted Rita. "But I think we'd all like to know what Roddy came up with."

"Thank you, Rita, I'll tell you.

"I tried to think whether there was anything in

what Bertie Watt-Knott was able to tell me about the things Kimpoo had been saying to White and Wong that could have any connection with the disappearance of the Colonel and Lady P."

"And did you find any connection?"

"Yes, I think I may have done. You see, Kimpoo was talking about some person or persons they were expecting, and I started to wonder if those two people might have been the Colonel and Lady P."

"But Roddy, if they were in White and Wong's offices, surely we'd have heard them today on the stuff you have had installed on our desks," said Lisa.

"True, Lisa, but only if they were in those rooms adjacent to our offices. You remember we heard Kimpoo come in from some door before he started talking in Hambonian to them."

"Yes, you're right, Roddy, and it did not sound like the front door because their buzzer did not go off. So it must have been a door to another part of their offices."

"Right so we know there is at least one other room, which we have not got bugged, and there may be more. But I have another thought. Many of these buildings here have basements and I am wondering if this building has one too."

"So there might be rooms under their offices."

"Precisely, and what's more, if there is a basement it might run underneath our own offices too. "

"Yes, I think you're probably right," said Rita. "If the Israeli consulate is anything to go by there is a basement that runs under the whole building, but there is only one place where you can get down to it. That's from the

103

stairs that lead down from the cipher clerk's office."

"So the same thing might apply to the building where we have moved into, and the only way down to the basement might be from the room at the back of White and Wong's office, the room that Kimpoo came out of."

"Heavens, Roddy, I think you could well be right," said Myra, but how are we going to find out? And what can we do, even if we do find out?"

"I intend to find out this very evening," said Roddy. "I have asked Bertie to send us the same two technicians who bugged White and Wong's offices for us. They should get here any time now. In fact I think I can hear them now."

Sure enough there was a knock on the door of the apartment. Myra went to the door and one of the techies came in. He explained that his mate was in the van outside and did not want to leave it unattended as they had brought a lot of equipment with them.

"Well. I want to make sure that White and Wong are not in their offices first, so I'll just phone them."

He phoned and there was no response.

"I think the coast is clear so we will go quietly and get into our own offices now. Any of you want to come with me?"

They all indicated they wanted to come, so they got into Roddy's SUV and followed by the techies in their van, they drove to the office. Roddy made a quick recce, so see that there were no lights coming from White and Wong's offices and then they all went as quietly as possible into Roddy's office.

The Dominatrix

By the time they all got to Roddy's office and the technicians had unloaded all their equipment from the van it was about 9.30 p.m. In the business district of Hangkow, where the office was located, all was quiet. In Hangkow very few people stayed on in their offices after about 6 p.m. and the streets in the office district tended to be deserted. Roddy phoned the local branch of Pizza Plus and ordered three large Super Sublime Whopper pizzas to be delivered along with soft drinks. When the pizza delivery man came to the door, Lisa and Myra met him and took the food and drinks from him and paid and tipped him. He did not step inside the office at all.

While Roddy, the Angels and the technicians had their informal picnic evening meal, Roddy outlined to the two technicians what he wanted. He realized that what he wanted might present some difficulties but the two men were experts in their rather unusual craft and told him they thought they could manage to give him what he wanted. One of them then got down on hands and knees and started crawling about the office, from time to time stopping and listening with a stethoscope to the floor. After a while the technician who seemed to be the boss of the team said, "Well, you are quite right. There is a basement below this room and I think the best place to start would be about here." He pointed to an area about a yard away from the wall.

"Shall I go ahead?'

"Yes, please do," said Roddy.

The two men then began to make a hole in the floor, rather similar to the holes they had previously made in the walls of Roddy's and Lisa's offices. The three women and Roddy were amazed at how quietly the two men did their work, they used special drills equipped with silencers and electric saws that were equally noiseless. After a while the senior technician said "We're almost through to the ceiling below, so please nobody talk. We cannot run the risk of anyone who might be down below hearing the slightest noise that would make them look up to the ceiling."

The room became uncannily quiet. The women and Roddy saw the two men working over the hole they had made with what looked more like surgical implements than electronic engineers' tools. The men placed equipment in the space they had made, then they covered it all up with some sort of packaging material. Finally, they got up off the ground and the senior man said to Roddy.

"Before we cover this up we need to fix the receiver into your computer." They then proceeded to partially dismantle the computer on Roddy's desk and inserted some new very small items in it. They then put it all together again and the senior man said, "Now let me just check that it is working."

He went to Roddy's computer and turned it on. He made some key strokes and a rather dim image appeared on the monitor screen. Although it was very dim they could make out a kind of stool, rather like the bench pianists sit on at a piano. There also appeared to be something rather shiny on the ground around the bench-like object.

"OK," he said. "That's about as good an image as we're going to get now, as there are obviously no lights on down there. But it's enough to show that the equipment is working well. Now, sir, let me show you how to work this."

He spent the next half an hour explaining to Roddy and Lisa exactly how to work the equipment, He explained that he had placed a tiny lens in the ceiling below that was hardly detectable.

"They'll probably mistake it for a small insect if they should see it all" he said. Then he went on to explain that the focal length could be adjusted so that in effect it became a zoom lens able to focus in on a close up of a small area to show or to expand the view so that almost all of the basement below could be seen. The field of view could be controlled from the computer. He also explained that the battery he had put in would probably last them for a month before it needed to be recharged, and he gave them a spare battery and showed them how to change the batteries and how to recharge them if necessary. He also told them that if they were viewing and listening in to what was going on down stairs it was very unlikely that the people down below could hear them.

"I've made it all as sound proof as possible," he

said, "but if they do hear any reflection of their own voices they'll probably just think it is some kind of echo. Oh, and by the way, I should get a carpet to put over this area so that no one sees that you have a funny little trapdoor in your floor." He then closed the hinged door at the top of the hole and locked it. He gave Roddy and Lisa each a key.

"Well, that's it then. I hope it gets you what you want. Me and my mate need to get back to Pispot now. We have another urgent job down there tomorrow."

Roddy thanked the two men profusely for their work and they left.

The screen was still on showing the dim view of the basement and Roddy said, "I might as well turn it off now. I doubt that we're going to see anything more tonight."

But just at that moment the screen brightened. Someone must have turned the light on downstairs. Then the four observers saw a very strange sight, Colonel Fairfax, totally naked but still struggling was brought into view. He was being carried in by Kimpoo and Mr Wong, who placed him face downwards over the bench and then tied him down so that there were chains attached to his arms and legs which in turn had their other ends attached to the bright objects they had seen on the basement floor and which turned out to be metal rings on the floor. They then left him there. The Colonel, although seemingly in a drugged and less than fully conscious state, was swearing and pleading with them, but they paid him no notice.

Just then an extraordinary vision came into their field of view. It was a tall woman clad only in a thong and knee length high heeled leather boots. She was holding a whip. She wore a black domino mask on her face, but her identity was unmistakable. As she strode towards the unfortunate colonel, she said in a loud voice. "I hear you've been a naughty boy."

"My God," said Lisa, "It's Lady P."

A Naughty Boy's Confession

Tied and face down as he was the Colonel gave a start as he heard the voice.

"Is that you, Mary? Thank God you've come. Please get me out of here."

The dominatrix cracked her whip.

"You will address me as Mistress Betty," she said, "and you will do exactly what I tell you to do and you will answer all my questions truthfully."

"All right, all right, I will do whatever you say, but for God's sake get me out of here." There was desperation in the Colonel's voice. But the reply he received brought him no comfort.

"I said you will address me as Mistress Betty." She cracked the whip again.

"OK, I'll call you Mistress Betty if you want but get me out of here."

"You miserable sniveling little toad. You don't seem to understand the situation."

This time the whip lashed the colonel's torso causing him to yell out in pain and bringing up a bloody red welt. His body appeared to go limp.

In Roddy's office upstairs, Myra said "I don't think I can stand to watch this. It is the cruelest form of torture."

"Well, I frankly don't see what we can do to help the Colonel, and I want to hear what she is going to ask him and what he says in reply" said Roddy.

"You know something?" said Rita. "You know those colored postcards that call girls get stuck up on the walls of the phone boxes in London advertising their services."

"You mean those pictures of semi or totally naked women with big boobs and words like 'Busty Blonde Bombshell' and a telephone number?" said Lisa. "They have people going round and sticking them up in the phone boxes in the evening and then the local council people have to go round taking them down again, but there are always enough of them on view in nearly all the phone boxes in the center of London."

"Yes, that's right. Well, I remember when I was in London some years ago, and, mind you, this was some years after Little Lizzie Squires had disappeared from the stage, – well, I remember seeing cards with the pictures of a tall woman with a whip and a black mask, and the words, as far as I can remember them, were 'Been a naughty boy? Call Mistress Betty for a lesson' and then a phone number. That must have been her!"

"My God, I believe you're right." said Roddy. "how could she have fallen so low!"

"Well, at any rate I'll give her credit for one thing," said Rita. "She's kept her figure pretty well. She still looks pretty good considering her age."

While this conversation was going on Roddy's eyes were still focused on the monitor.

The colonel appeared to have passed out. Roddy used the zoom control to enlarge the view of the area down below. He saw that about twenty to twenty-five feet away from the bench over which the Colonel was chained, there were two chairs. Wong sat in one of them and Kimpoo in the other. The dominatrix strode over to them.

"You'd better bring him round," she said, "We can't afford to give him a heart attack and let him die."

Kimpoo got up and came back with a bucket of water which he threw over the colonel's body. The colonel stirred. He sounded as if he were crying.

The dominatrix strode over to him again,

"Are you ready to answer some questions now?"

"Yes."

"Say 'Yes, Mistress Betty.'"

"Yes, Mistress Betty."

She cracked her whip again.

"You better answer my questions truthfully or you'll have to answer to Willie. Willie, can really hurt people, can't you Willie?"

"Who's Willie?" asked the colonel in a hoarse voice.

"Willie's my whip and he doesn't like people who do not address me as Mistress Betty."

She passed the whip over the colonel's bare body. He winced but this time she did not flay him.

"You had better say 'Sorry'" to Mistress Betty.

"I'm sorry, Mistress Betty," responded a defeated and despondent sounding Colonel.

"Now tell Mistress Betty this, you naughty boy. Did you poison Mr Gospodinov?"

"How could you believe such a thing, Mary?" cried the Colonel.

There was a crack of the whip and a scream from the Colonel.

"Answer the question. Willie is getting impatient."

She cracked the whip again.

"Mistress Betty is waiting."

"Yes, I put poison in his drink."

"That's a good boy. Now tell Mistress Betty why you killed him."

"For God's sake, he was getting suspicious of me."

"All right, you naughty boy, we can put the rest of the story together quite easily."

At that point the dominatrix appeared to be exchanging signals with Mr Wong.

"And did you poison the croissant that I gave you to give to the Consul General, Devenish?"

"You know damn well I did.

"But you tried to put suspicion on Lady Ponsonby, didn't you, you foul little toad?"

The whip flashed again and a piercing shriek came from the colonel.

Upstairs Myra was getting increasingly agitated.

"Roddy, we have got to stop this somehow. The wretched man is going to be tortured to death if we don't do something."

To the Rescue

"You're right," agreed Lisa, "but how can we get into the basement to rescue him?"

"Hold your horses a moment," said Roddy. "Of course, we will try to save the old bastard's life. But until we can get into the basement we need to keep watching and recording what is going on downstairs. Thank God the technician did show me how to keep all this recorded in the memory of the computer."

"You mean we will have a record of all this?" asked Myra.

"Yes, I started recording as soon as 'Mistress Betty' appeared."

"That figures" said Myra, somewhat grimly.

"Anyway I will go down and see how we can get into the basement, but I want you to stay here, Liza, keeping the recording going. Even when and if we get in there I think we had better have it all recorded, but once we are in there I'll be able to send you messages through the bug we have down there."

Roddy went through with Liza how to control the recording.

Then he turned to Myra and Rita.

"I suggest you two come with me."

"Good," said Myra, "I couldn't go on watching the colonel being tortured, terrible man that he is."

Leaving Liza behind the three of them left the office.

"I suggest we go round to the back and see if we can find a way in there," said Roddy.

Around the back of the building they came to a heavy steel doorway painted green. There was no handle of any kind on it nor was there any key hole. Roddy went to his SUV and got out a tire lever from the tool box he carried in it. He came back to the door where the two women were waiting. With the tire lever he tried to jemmy the door open, but the door did not budge.

"Looks like we'll have to try the front entrance. It seems this can only be opened from the inside."

They all went round to the front of the building. The entrances to Roddy's offices and those of White and Wong were side by side.

"Well, I don't think it would do any good to ring the bell," said Myra. "They aren't likely to open the door to us and we'll only put them on their guard."

"You're right as usual, my love," said Roddy. "I'll tell you what we are going to do. I want you to get in the SUV, Myra, and I want you to ram the door to their offices so that we can break in."

"But won't you smash the door to your own offices too?"

"Not if you drive in from the right angle. I'm going to stand by the lawyers' office door and give you very careful directions. When I think we have the angle just right I want you to put your foot down and crash into the door. Better make sure you're wearing your seat belt."

Myra got into the driver's seat of the SUV and drove close to the doors of the two offices. Roddy made her do quite a bit of maneuvering until he was sure she could smash open the door to White and Wong's office without damaging the door to Roddy's office suite. When Roddy gave her the signal she crashed into the door and backed quickly out again. Roddy dashed through the door followed immediately by Rita. Myra followed them as soon as she could get out of the SUV.

In a moment all three were in the office where Roddy had met with the two lawyers before. At the back of the room there were two doors. Roddy ran to one and Rita to the other. Both were locked. Without hesitating Roddy took an automatic out of his shoulder holster and shot out the lock of the door in front of him. He opened the door and found himself in a small pantry equipped with a micro oven. He withdrew and went immediately over to the door which Rita had gone to and repeated the same action with his automatic. This door opened into another office with copying machines and other office equipment in it. At the back of this room was another door. This time Roddy just felt the door handle to see if the door was locked. As he expected, it was, so he shot out that lock too. Behind this door there were steps going down. With his gun still held in his right hand he went down these steps with the two women close behind him. At the bottom of the steps he looked around and saw three people seated behind a table, the two lawyers and "Mistress Betty" now more modestly clad with a black silk negligee over the rather spare clothing that they had seen her wearing on the compuer monitor.

"Ah," said Mr White smiling, " You do have a rather dramatic, not to say expensive way of dropping in to see old friends, don't you, Group Captain?"

Murphy's Law and some Clearing of the Air

"Where's the Colonel?" demanded Roddy.

"What are you talking about?" responded,Mr Wong.

Roddy did not wait any further. He rushed past the table to a door behind them. It was of course locked.

"Please don't start shooting again", said Mr White. "You've given me a headache.

"Here, take this key. You can open the door and see for yourself. But I don't think you'll find anyone there."

Roddy inserted the key and unlocked the door. He went through. The room beyond was in total darkness. He felt along the wall until he found a light switch. He switched on the lights.

"Oh, my God," he yelled out. "He's killed him."

At this point all the others, the lawyers, Lady P, Rita and Myra came rushing to the door and into the room.

The sight they saw was not at all what they expected. The bleeding body of Kimpoo was on the floor, but there was no sign of the colonel.

"What the hell has happened?" asked Mr White rather rhetorically.

He looked at Mr Wong who said "He can't have gone far in the state he's in. I'll just go upstairs and phone our friends to look for him and pick him up."

"It's all the fault of that bloody stupid secret agent." Lady P spat out the words with venom. "He thinks he's James bloody Bond. He even has himself surrounded by sexy women."

"Cool down everyone" said the calm voice of Mr White. I think we had better go upstairs and we can all discuss the situation. "Murphy's law seems to have struck again, just as we thought we were getting somewhere."

Roddy turned his face up towards the ceiling and said in a loud voice. "You can turn things off now, Lisa. I think you had better come and join us in Wong and White's office."

A few minutes later all concerned were sitting in the main office of White and Wong. Lady Ponsonby, alias Mistress Betty, was still fuming but all the others were by now relatively cool.

"May we ask you to start, Group Captain? I would like to know what made you come literally crashing into our offices just now."

Roddy explained without holding much information back. He related how he had had the lawyer's offices bugged and how he had had the magic eye inserted in the ceiling of their basement.

"So we saw what Lady Ponsonby in her Mistress Betty garb was doing to the colonel and we were afraid she was going to kill him."

Lady P sat up very straight in her chair. "You stupid little man," she said. "Do you think I don't know my business? Mind you, it would not have been any great loss if he had died, but I wasn't going to do anything to finish him off, at least until I had got all the information we needed from him."

"And what did you find out?"

"I don't know how much you have on your dammed recording, but we had just got the name of the organization he was working for."

"And what was that?"

"Look," Lady P turned to Mr Wong. "Do I really have to give this incompetent amateur the information that he himself has miserably failed to gather."

"I think you had better, Betty," replied Mr Wong. "He has after all displayed some initiative in putting together what we have been doing."

"Oh, all right, but I'm not going to address him as Group Captain, a title to which he is in no way entitled. I doubt if the silly bastard can even fly a plane."

In spite of the insults from Lady P, Roddy smiled. "You are quite right, Lady Ponsonby. I have never flown a conventional aircraft in my life, but I am pretty good with helicopters. I flew one in the Falklands war."

Mr White nodded, "That's right, Betty," he said, "he did fly helicopters. That was during the Falklands war. But he was Major Jack McKayLean then. Isn't that true?"

Roddy nodded, and then asked, "And are you really entitled to call yourself Lady Ponsonby."

"Yes, I bloody well am."

"And since we're all being truthful now, your

ladyship, tell me, did you murder your husband."

"No, I did not. I was actually quite fond of the silly old bugger. Unfortunately he did get a bit over excited one day when we were playing some erotic games. Before we were married he was a client of Mistress Betty's. And he had a collection of all my films."

"Oh," broke in Rita, "so it was you who made those porno films in the series 'Mistress Betty and the Naughty Boys?' We used to get hold of copies and play them on the school's equipment when no one was about."

"Disgraceful. And I never made porno films," said Lady P indignantly. "I made erotic films. I would never do hard core. I despise and detest the stuff."

"We seem to be getting away from the point of this gathering," interrupted Mr White. "Can we get back to what we found out from the colonel.?

"Yes, we will in a minute" said Lady P, still sounding imperious. "But first there are still a few things I'd like to clear up. First, Myra, are you married to this man with all the various names and ranks."

"Yes."

"If that is so, you were also Mrs Bloggs. And that means he was also Sid Bloggs?"

"That is correct." agreed Myra.

"Well, I have to congratulate you there." She actually smiled at Roddy. "I would never have realized it. But there's one more thing. Rita, you are not Mossad, are you?"

"No, I'm not."

"How did you come to be mixed up with this lot."

"I am just an old buddy of Myra's. In fact you and she and I might get together and found an East End Jewess's association."

"Oh my God, then you remember Little Lizzie Squires. I was good wasn't I."

"Yes, you were very good."

"And, Lisa, how do you fit in? You're his secretary aren't you?"

"Yes."

"And are you anything beyond that."

"What do you mean."

" I am not talking about anything sexual – though you never know with these SIS boys. I mean are you a part of the intelligence community?"

"Sort of. I am actually involved with MI5, checking on the internal security of the British diplomatic and consular offices in Hambonia."

"Good Lord," said Roddy, "That's what I have suspected, but I really did not know until now."

"Well, now we seem to know who we all are, so we can get back to the subject of our interrogation of the colonel," said Mr Wong.

"Hold on a moment. I have a question," said Roddy. "First, how did you get involved with Mossad, Lady Ponsonby; and secondly how exactly do you fit into all this?"

"Well, in my days as Mistress Betty, I had a number of Arab gentlemen as my clients. One day I was approached by a member of the Israeli embassy in London and he asked me if I could just keep my eyes and ears open and report to him from time to time. That's how it started. And that's how I first came in contact with

Colonel Fairfax. He seemed to be involved in some way with several of the Arab gentlemen I knew."

"Okay, now Mr Wong, would you or Mr White explain your involvement? You told me you worked for Canadian intelligence."

"Yes, we do," said Mr White. "But we are given a good deal of leeway to work with other services including those of our neighbor to the South. It was those guys I was on the phone to. They'll pick up the colonel soon, I'm sure."

"For goodness sake," said Roddy. "The last thing we want is for him to fall into the CIA's hands. They'll ship him off to Guantanamo Bay or somewhere and we'll never see him again."

"Yes, and I don't think their interrogation methods are as good as mine," agreed Lady P. "We've got to get hold of him before they can get him out of the country."

"Agreed" said Roddy. "But I want to know how he managed to kill Kimpoo and get away."

"I think I can guess that," said Lady P. "Kimpoo was being kept up in the penthouse on the roof for two reasons. One, he was being given training as an agent, and two, we were in some doubt as to whether he might be a double."

"You mean you think he might have been in touch with the CIA?"

"Yes, but why would they kill him?"

"Good question, but do you think he might have let them in through the back door, and that they took the colonel out that way?"

"Yes, I do. While you were crashing into the place and causing a major distraction, they could easily have done so."

"In that case we've got to find him and get him back into our hands as soon as possible."

Who is Kimpoo?

"Just a minute before everyone goes running off looking for the Colonel, don't forget there's a dead man lying in the place over there," interrupted Myra in her usual down to earth and practical manner.

"You're right," agreed Mr Wong. "We can't just leave him there, and there's no way we're going to bring the police in here. We're going to have to dispose of his body somehow."

The whole group trooped back to the door to the space where they had left the corpse and through the door. Mr White was the first person through the door. He stopped.

"My God, he's gone too."

The bloody clothes that Kimpoo had been wearing were in a neat pile on the floor, but of the corpse there was no trace.

"Just a moment" said Roddy. "Just let me have a look at those clothes." He picked up the bloody shirt and held it close to his nose, then he put his finger on one of the bloodiest patches of the shirt and then touched his tongue. He started laughing.

"I thought they only did this in movies."

"What do you mean?'

"Have you never heard of using tomato ketchup to simulate blood? Don't you see what happened. We were so taken aback by seeing what we thought was a bloody corpse that we never even stopped to examine it closely. We've been completely duped. My guess is that Kimpoo is in excellent health and has cleared off. But where to? Has anybody any ideas about that."

"I think," said Myra, "that we need to ask Lady Ponsonby about that. You've been working for Mossad, so you should know."

"Well, to tell the truth," replied Lady P, "I really don't know much about him. I know he was being trained as an agent for Mossad, and I knew there were suspicions about his loyalty. I was told that he was to accompany me here, where I was to interrogate the Colonel, and I was told to keep a very careful eye on him. But that's really all I know about him."

"Really?" asked Myra skeptically.

"You know, love, I think she's telling the truth," said Roddy.

"Of course, I'm telling the truth, young lady," said Lady P, returning to her usual imperious mode of speech. "You ought to know. You worked for Mossad yourself. Everything is on a need to know basis. No one tells you the whole story. One agent may know nothing about what another is doing. I know no more about Kimpoo than I have told you."

"Do you even know if he is a Hambonian," asked Mr Wong.

"Not really. I assumed he was because he spoke the language. Does it matter?"

"It might. If he really is a Hambonian someone might realize he has gone missing and start making inquiries, and we don't want that. But on the other hand if he is an illegal alien from one of the neighboring countries with a language similar to the Hambonian language, that's a different matter."

"Well, I don't see how we can find anything about that now" said Roddy."The question is what are we to do now? We don't really have any idea where the Colonel is. It seems most likely that Kimpoo helped him get out of here, but he must also have had help from other people outside. Then Kimpoo must have changed his clothes and got away himself, but whether he has gone to the same destination as the colonel we have no means of knowing."

"In fact" said Lisa, "we seem to have screwed things up royally."

"Yes, you have," said Lady Ponsonby by now extremely angry. "If you had not all come bursting in when you did, I would have got all the information we wanted from the stupid old bastard."

"I'm not so sure about that" retorted Myra, "It's more likely you'd have killed him."

"Shut up, you little trollop, I am a highly experienced expert in these matters, and I know exactly what I was doing."

"Well," said Rita, "he may have been a villain, but we are supposed to be civilized people and civilized people have some respect for human rights. They don't go about torturing people almost or maybe completely to death."

"I don't give a shit for the human rights of people

like him. He had no regard for the human rights of people in Israel. He was selling them out for money and depriving the Israeli people of the weapons they needed and, mind you, had paid for, to defend themselves from the bloody Arabs."

"You're very sure of this?" asked Roddy.

"Of course, I'm bloody sure. I was just trying to find out who was paying him, when you lot came in and ruined everything."

At this point Mr White got up on a chair and shouted in a very loud voice. "Shut up all of you. This is getting us nowhere. We have to start from where we are. What I would like to know is, do we all have the same interest in getting the information from the Colonel that Lady Ponsonby was trying to get out of him, and secondly can we all agree to work together for that purpose? I suggest we all sit down and all keep quiet for two minutes, Then we can discuss in a civilized manner what we should do next."

"I agree with Mr White," said Roddy, "but I think we should add one thing to what he has said."

"What's that""

"I think we need to find out exactly who and what Mr Kimpoo is and how he fits into the larger picture."

"Agreed."

The whole group, Lady Ponsonby, White and Wong, Roddy and the three angels, Myra, Rita and Lisa sat solemnly for the next two minutes, each one thinking his or her own thoughts and wondering at the same time what was going on in the minds of the others.

Part 4

The Cashiered Quartermaster

Where is the Colonel?

In London, in New York and Washington, even in Paris, Brussels, Rome and Berlin, as well of course in Hambonia, newspapers carried the story of the mysterious disappearance of the acting British Consul General in Hangkow. CNN International dispatched its resident reporter in Pispot to go to Hangkow to interview the distinguished English resident, Lady Ponsonby who was known to be a close friend of the missing diplomat, but her ladyship was only able to describe her complete amazement at the Consul General's disappearance. But it was clear to the viewers that the aristocratic lady seemed to be enjoying her appearance on international television, and she gave interviews later to the BBC, Fox news, and MSNBC. Larry King even conducted a long distance interview with her on Larry King Live.

The British Foreign Office and the British authorities on the spot in Hambonia were however very close mouthed and would only comment that the matter of the Colonel's disappearance was under active investigation and that they were following up various leads. The Inspector General of the Hambonian National Police Force was interviewed and merely commented that he

had not been informed of the Consul's disappearance
and that therefore the police were in no position to take
any action.

Even the former Regimental Quarter Master
Sergeant Tony Fairfax, who had been dishonorably
discharged from the British army, but who was now
generally known as Colonel Fairfax, did not know
where he was himself. He could remember passing out
in agony in the basement of the offices of the law firm
of White and Wong. He could remember the terrible
and brutal whipping he had received from the woman
who had been his mistress and who he had thought of
as a friend. It was true that the sex games they sometimes
used play were apt to get a little rough, but he had
never suspected her. Now it seemed she was a Jewish
secret agent. How could he have been duped by her?

He vaguely remembered waking up in an aircraft
bound for he knew not where. He remembered the kind
face of an elderly doctor who spoke to him in Arabic.
He had told him that he had been very badly wounded
and that partly as a result of the severe wounds he had
sustained he had had a nearly fatal heart attack. Then
the doctor had sedated him.

When he woke again he realized he was in a hospital.
He also realized that his body was still extremely
painful. Soon he was asleep again.

The next time he woke a few more memories
came back to him. He remembered a man they had
called Kimpoo, He had taken him to be a Hambonian as
he spoke the language. He seemed to remember the
man being present on the ghastly occasion when he was
almost killed by that mad bitch with the whip. He

drifted off into another troubled sleep.

When he finally became fully conscious he looked around the room he was in. It appeared to be a rather high class hospital room. He tried to get out of bed, but the agony of his body prevented him. On an electronic panel besides his bed he noticed a button marked "Bell." He pressed it. A uniformed nurse came in, looked at him and quickly went out of the room again. He shouted after her. Then the door opened again and the man called Kimpoo came into the room.

"Oh, good. I see you are feeling better."

"I'm feeling bloody awful. But tell me, where in Hell's name am I?"

"You're in a safe place. This is a hospital run by your friends."

"Who the Hell are you anyway? You were there when they were torturing me."

"Yes, I was there. I had to be. But it was also me who got you out of that place into a place of safety. There is much I can tell you when you feel well enough to talk."

"Well, we can start now. First of all who are you?"

"My name is Abdul Hussein Kimpoo."

"Thats an odd name. Are you a Muslim Hambonian? I didn't think there were any."

"You see my father was Hambonian but my mother is Palestinan from Gaza. They met at University in Delhi. My father converted to Islam and after graduating they both went to Palestine to visit my mother's family."

"I see you used the past tense when referring to you father. Is he dead then?"

"Yes, he was killed by an Israeli bomb, one of the many innocent civilians killed by Israeli bombing."

"I'm sorry. How old were you at the time."

"I had not been born. My mother was pregnant at the time, but I was born prematurely soon after his death. It was the shock that my mother suffered from my father's death that caused her to go into labor prematurely."

"I see. So you have no love for the Israelis then?"

"I have every reason to hate them."

"What happened after that."

"When my mother considered that I was old enough to travel with her she took me to live with her in France. She had relatives there. But she also got in touch with members of the Hambonian residents there. She felt she owed it to my father to make sure I understood my Hambonian heritage as well as the Palestinian one. I had to learn to speak the language. At a very young age it is easy to learn a language and by the time I was twelve I could speak the language like a native speaker, which of course I really was."

"Do you also speak Arabic.?"

"Oh, yes. My mother made sure of that. You see I had to speak Hambonian with the members of the expatriate Hambonian community, French at school, and Arabic at home with my mother."

"My! My! You are quite a linguist aren't you. But now you are speaking English to me. How did you pick that up?"

"As I told you, it is easy to learn a language if you start when you are young. I had no trouble picking up English, but I do not speak it as well as I do the other languages. When I talk to you, I do not sound like an Englishman, do I?"

"Not like anyone I have ever met. But tell me how did you get mixed up in all this ……. this bloody business."

"It's a bit of a tall story – I'm sorry. I should say a long story. But I see that you are getting tired. Would you like some food or drink? I can tell the nurse to bring you something."

"Perhaps something to drink."

"OK, I'll have the nurse bring you something."

Kimpoo left the room and shortly afterwards a nurse came in with a tray of food for the colonel. The Colonel who was still mildly sedated, returned to his slumbers, which were filled with alarming dreams.

The next morning a nurse woke him to give him some pills to take and a rather unpleasant small glass of liquid to drink. The colonel ate some solid food for the first time since he had been admitted to the hospital. A little later Kimpoo came in to see him.

"What's the time, Kimpoo? There's no clock in this room and I don't seem to have a watch any more."

"I really don't think you should worry too much about the time of day, Tony – may I call you Tony? The first thing is to get your strength back. You know you had a nearly fatal heart attack?"

"Yes, that doctor told me that. But how long have I got to stay in this hospital? Nobody tells me anything. I don't even know how long I've been here."

"I really don't know how long you'll be here, Tony. You have to get fit again and you are going to have to answer some questions."

"Bloody Hell, What do you mean? Me answer questions?. I want some answers not bloody questions."

"Well, Tony, surely you must realize that no one really trusts you. You are a crook. You were thrown out of the British army because you were selling army equipment. You were in fact very lucky not to have gone to jail for a long time. But you seemed to have some sympathy with the Arab cause, so your friends helped you. But you are a man who betrayed his own country not once, but several times and in many ways. So how do your present friends know that you won't betray them?"

At the end of Kimpoo's remarks the Colonel at first looked furious and then seemed to crumple as he realized the desperately tight spot he was in. He was virtually a prisoner in this unknown hospital. He had no resources, not even any clothes and he did not even know what country he was in. He was completely in the power of whoever it was who had brought him to this place. He was quiet for some minutes and Kimpoo sat in a chair by his bed saying nothing. At last the Colonel sat up a bit more firmly in this bed and asked Kimpoo.

"What on earth were you doing in that cellar where they were torturing me? And why did you help to get me away from there?"

Kimpoo smiled, "Ah, Tony, I can answer that. I had infiltrated the Israeli secret service and they were trying to train me to work as an agent for them, but I guess I must have slipped up at some point in my dealings with them as they were beginning to suspect me of being a double. I think it was to test me that they sent me to work with the woman you knew as Lady

Ponsonby. They told me that I was to take part in an
interrogation of an agent of an Arab terrorist group. So I
had to go along to the offices of White and Wong. It was
lucky for you that the group of British agents came
crashing into the place and I was able to get you out of
the place. You see I had tipped off my friends what was
happening, so they were waiting outside the back entrance of the cellar to White and Wong's place. While all
the disturbance was going on White and Wong and the
Lady rushed out of the place and I was able to let my
friends in and they took you out and eventually they
brought you and me both here. But it was touch and go.
I did not have time to get out of that basement myself,
so I managed to look as if I had been murdered, and
they went out again."

"You had to make it look as if you had been murdered? How the Hell did you do that?"

Kimpoo laughed. "That was the easy part. I kept
a bottle of what looked like blood. It was actually
tomato ketchup. It's true that I ruined my clothes but I
spread the ketchup liberally over my chest and
shammed death. They were completely taken in. They
must have got quite a shock when they came back to
find me gone."

"Good God, Kimpoo. Seems to me you must have
had a pretty good training as an agent."

Kimpoo laughed again, "You're quite right, Tony.
I got most of my training in Pakistan, but then later I
received more training from the Israelis and managed to
use that against them."

"But Kimpoo, you mentioned these friends of
yours who whisked us both out of harm's way. Tell me

who are they?"

"I'm sorry, Tony. That is something that you do not need to know." Kimpoo got up and walked out of the room.

The Colonel did not see Kimpoo again for two days. Although he was not aware of the fact, he was being thoroughly sedated, so that he would make no move to get out of the hospital. When Kimpoo did come in to see him again, the Colonel, who was feeling a little more alert, asked him agitatedly.

"Please Kimpoo, can you at least tell me where I am and how long I am going to have to stay in this hospital?"

Kimpoo smiled a rather grim smile.

"Be happy you are here, Tony. This is a very good hospital, never mind its exact location. Believe me, Tony, you don't want to know about the treatment you might be getting, if certain people had had their way."

"What do you mean?"

"I mean, Tony, that nobody trusts you. You betrayed your own country when you were in the British army, so there's no guarantee you would not betray anyone else who employed you. That's the penalty you pay for being a traitor, Tony. Nobody trusts you, nobody!"

The Colonel spluttered but had no response he could make. For a few minutes there was quiet in the room. Finally Kimpoo broke it.

"My advice to you, Tony, is to be a good boy and do exactly what the people who have you in their hands now tell you to do."

"But Kimploo I have been carrying out exactly what the AAAI was asking me to do."

"You mean what the Arab Alliance Against Infidels was paying you to do, don't you, Tony."

"Yes, all right. So I suppose its them who arranged my rescue and are holding me here. What more do they want?"

"Tony, you're a bit slow in the uptake. I suppose its because of the sedatives you've been given. But let me assure you, the AAAI have no idea where you are and they probably believe that you have gone over to the Israelis because of your liaison with the remarkable Lady Ponsonby."

"But how could they think that? It was only recently I got rid of Gospodinov for them and arranged the diversion of the arms meant for Israel."

"Exactly, Tony, keep the murder of Gospodinov in your mind. The British intelligence people know all about that and if you show your face you will almost certainly face a trial for murder. Secondly, Tony, what makes you sure that those Russian arms actually reached your friends?"

"Oh, my God, Kimpoo, are you telling me they never did?"

"Well, Tony, let's just suppose that there was a second diversion. Your friends would not be too pleased about that, would they? They might take it into their heads that you had arranged it, perhaps through your good friend Lady P."

"Kimpoo, for God's sake, I am getting really confused now. You seem to be telling me that somebody hijacked the arms shipment after I had diverted it from the Israelis, and that possibly Lady P did it. So now the AAAI guys are after my head, but who are you working for? It can't be the Israelis, since it was you that got me out of the vicious hands of that murdering bitch, and it can't be the

AAAI, but you tell me you work for the Palestinian cause, so who or what are you really?"

Kimpoo smiled. "Think of it as a Sudoku puzzle, Tony, and try to work it out for yourself. It will give you something to do while you are here in this beautiful hospital."

Roddy and the Angels Want to Know.

Immediately after the disappearances of the Colonel and of Kimpoo, Myra, the ever practical one, asked, "Can anyone tell me what the hell is going on?"

Roddy took up from there. "Yes, I think there is a lot of explaining to be done. Let's start with you, Mr White and Mr Wong. How come you seem to be working with Mossad on this caper? From all I can gather you are genuinely members of the Canadian secret service. How are you involved?"

Mr White looked at Mr Wong, who nodded. "Everything we have told you," he said, "is the truth. If you remember I told you we have been here for a long time now and our HQ seemed almost to have forgotten us, but they left us here as sleepers. Our law work took most of our time, but we were more or less left to our own initiatives when it came to intelligence matters. Dealing with the Colonel's legal affairs, we began to suspect that he was engaged in clandestine activities. When we investigated his background, we found the same things that you did. He is basically a crook and a traitor, but he has spent much of his working life with middle eastern armies. We thought he might be working with one of the illegal military organization in the Arab world, one of the terrorist orgaizations in fact."

"Yes," Mr White took up the tale. "So it made sense to us to pass on our suspicions to a friendly sister agency."

"You mean Mossad?"

"Precisely. They wanted to interrogate the Colonel and we agreed it could be done in our basement here. As you will have seen, Lady Ponsonby is highly skilled as an interrogator."

"That's not exactly what I would have called her," muttered Myra under her breath.

"All was going well until you came crashing in."

"Excuse me," interrupted Lisa. "I can tell you that things were not going well. If we had not bust in, the Colonel would be dead. As a trained nurse I could see that the man was having a heart attack. One more lash of the whip would have finished him off."

"Oh," Mr Wong looked surprised. "Are you sure of that Major Goodbody?"

"Yes, I am virtually certain."

Mr Wong turned to Lady Ponsonby. "Lizzie, you swore to us that you knew exactly how much punishment a person could take."

"Well, I did not know he had such a weak heart. And I assure you I have extracted secrets from a large number of people without having any of them ever dying on me."

"Frankly, none of that makes much difference now," interjected Roddy. "The Colonel, as far as we know, did not die, though he must be in a pretty bad way. But God knows who has got hold of him and where he is now."

"If you ask me." said Lisa. "Assuming whoever has got him wants him to live, they will need to see that he gets expert medical treatment a.s.a.p. My guess is that they would get him as quickly as possible to a first class hospital, maybe one outside this country."

"That's an interesting thought, Lisa," agreed Roddy. "My guess would be that they would take him to Indonesia or Malaysia. They are the two Moslem countries in this region and most likely to be supportive of the Arab cause."

"OK. We'll follow that up, but there's something else we need to know more about, and that's this man they call Kimpoo. Do any of you know anything much about thim. How about you, Lady Ponsonby? He was supposed to be working with you."

"All I know is that he is a Hambonian, though I believe his mother was a foreigner. He had been re-cruited to be an agent for Mossad, but they his handlers were beginning to have suspicions about him. He was assigned to work with me on the interrogation of the Colonel. It was to be a kind of test for him. I was warned to keep a very careful eye on him. He gave no sign of causing any problems until you lot interrupted the interrogation."

"His mother was Palestinian," said Mr Wong. "I guess that's why your people were beginning to have suspicions about him."

"I have just remembered something," said Lady P. "When we were on our way over here, before the interrogation. He suggested we stop for a cup of coffee at the Starbucks in Hekman Plaza. So we did so and he seemed to take rather a long time ordering the coffees from the barista. He seemed to be talking much longer than it would have taken to order two cappuccinos. I guess he must have been talking to his contact on the other side."

"Yes, that could account for a lot of things." agreed Roddy. "I think we have done about as much as we can tonight, so why don't we all go home and sleep on things. But at least one thing is clear. It was the Colonel who murdered the Russian, Gospodinov. I am not sure what if anything we should do about that. I'll talk to the Colonel's replacement as Consul General in the morning."

The next morning Roddy and Myra arranged to meet with Rita and Lisa during Rita's lunch break, when she could get away from the Israeli consulate.

Rita began by remarking, "Roddy, last night you said that at least one thing was clear; that it was the Colonel who murdered that Russian fellow, Gospodinov. But surely there is a good deal more than that that we have learned. I mean we know for certain that Lady P is a Mossad agent, and we know that Kimpoo is working for some pro-Palestinian group."

"Well, you are almost certainly right about Kimpoo" agreed Roddy, but I am not quite so certain about Lady P."

"Why? What do you mean?"

"You remember she said she knew exactly what she was doing? When she was giving the Colonel a whipping?"

"Yes."

"Well I think she was probably telling the truth."

"You mean she knew she was almost killing the Colonel?"

"Yes, and I think she would have done so, if we had not intervened just in time."

"But if he had died, she would never have got the information from him about who he was getting his instructions from, who was the terrorist organization behind him."

"Exactly."

"But that would imply that she was a double agent, pretending to be working for Mossad but in reality making sure they did not get the information she was supposed to be getting from the Colonel."

"Right again, Lisa."

"Well, I guess you could well be right," agreed Rita, "and I don't believe that she was an actual regular Mossad agent, but rather that she was just being employed by Mossad for a particular job. I think I know all the Mossad people attached to the consulate, but I have never seen her there."

Thinking it over, I too think that Roddy is right," said Lisa. "She almost certainly knew that the Colonel had a rather weak heart. She also knew from the sex games she had played with him previously that he got very excited, when she did her thing as a dominatrix and gave him a whipping. So the sexual excitement would have raised the level of strain on his heart and then when she started to inflict real, severe pain on him, it could and it did cause him to have a heart attack."

"So you think she was an agent of an Arab extremist group."

"I think it is distinctly possible."

"But she is a Jew" objected Rita, "how could she bring herself to do such a thing."

"Well" said Myra, "the four of us know she was a Jew, but she never made herself a part of the Jewish community. Her late husband was not Jewish, and I vaguely remember photos of her wedding appearing in the Evening News. They showed she was married at St. Paul's cathedral. So I don't think she cared too much about the Jewish cause or about Israel."

"Sounds like she's a very devious person."

Part 5

The Big Bang

A Future Hero of the Revolution?

The Colonel was feeling much better. He still did not know where he was or even the name of the hospital where he was recuperating. He was allowed up and was allowed to walk to the common reading room on the same floor as his room. Kimpoo still came to visit him regularly.

One day the Colonel asked him, "I say Kimpoo, old boy, when am I going to get out of this place. I'm feeling quite fit again now and I am getting rather bored.

Kimpoo's reply was rather too vague for the Colonel's liking.

"Don't worry Tony. You'll soon be out of here. Our bosses have a vitally important task for you. I am quite envious. In fact Tony, if you can carry out this task successfully I think you may become one of the great heroes of the Palestinian resistance, a hero of the great revolution."

"That's all very well, Kimpoo. But first I need to be able to get out and about. Tell me where exactly am I? And what is this hospital?"

"I should not worry about that, Colonel. All will

be revealed to you when the time is ripe, but for the moment it is in your own best interests that you should not know."

The Colonel could get no more out of Kimpoo. He tried to figure it out for himself. The staff of the hospital that he met, the nurses, doctors and technicians did not give him much clue. One of his nurses looked like an Indian, another looked more Chinese, a third could have been a Malay. Then there was one who spoke with what sounded to him like an Italian accent. One of the doctors sounded and looked like an Englishman, but another left him guessing. He could have been Persian, Egyptian or God knows what, but he did not appear to be of European origin. One of the nurses, the one who looked Indian, had a gold chain with the OM sign in gold as a pendant. Another wore a cross. Yet aother wore a headscarf all the time and presumably was Muslim. It seemed to the Colonel that the hospital must be an international one, but where was it? He had not seen many of the patients but those he had seen seemed to be just as big a mix as the staff. Why the hell was Kimpoo being so bloody secretive about the location of the hospital?

It also worried the Colonel that he had no clothes of his own. The hospital provided him with pajamas and a dressing gown and slippers. But when he was abducted from the offices of White and Wong, he had been stark naked, so he had no clothes with him and Kimpoo had not brought any clothes for him to wear, so there was no way he could just walk out of the hospital.

And just what had Kimpoo meant when he had

told him that he would become a Hero of the Great Revolution. He had absolutely no desire to try to do anything heroic. Right now he just wanted a quiet life. He just wanted to get away to some quiet place where nobody knew him, and no one knew anything about his previous activities. But he realized that Kimpoo was just guarding him, And the hospital seemed to be in ka-hoots with Kimpoo in keeping him a prisoner. What the hell was going on?

Then one day Kimpoo came to see him accompanied by a man who looked South East Asian.

"Tony," said Kimpoo. "We need to get you some clothes and Mr Gafoo here has come to measure you for them. We will also need to get your neck size and we'll fit you out with a complete new outfit."

"And about time too," responded the Colonel, who was feeling greatly relieved.

The Greenpeace Connection

Rita phoned Roddy in great excitement.

"Roddy, can you and Myra meet me for lunch. Something that may be really important has just come up."

Roddy told Myra and Lisa.

Myra commented with a smile. "I am sure tongues must be wagging, Roddy."

"Why, love?"

"People must be wondering why the four of us are seen together so much. They must be thinking that you have a harem of your own with three wives."

"Well, it is a delightful idea now you've mentioned it," joked Roddy, "but I don't think I could afford it on my salary."

"Why nor? You could put your two extra wives down as expenses couldn't you?"

"No, I dont't think I could get away with that, Myra. I know that some of my colleagues do entertain ladies of the night and put them down as expenses, but I don't think I could get away with claiming for the living expenses of two extra women."

"Really, Roddy. Maybe I am naïve, but how do your colleagues claim these women as expenses?"

"They put them down as informers from whom they gain important information."

"Well," said Myra after giving the matter a moment's thought, "maybe they do."

"Sure," said Roddy. They both laughed.

At lunch Rita could hardly contain herself.

"You'll never believe what's happened."

"Tell us, Rita."

"Well. The Russians have just found some of the crates that the armaments Israel had bought from them had been shipped in."

"No, where did they find them."

Rita challenged them to guess, but none of them came up with the right answer. Roddy said "You're going to have to tell us Rita."

"They found them aboard a Greenpeace vessel. They had stopped it and boarded it as it had sailed too close to one of their nuclear sub bases. They searched the ship and found the crates. Of course there were no arms in them. They actually contained agriculrural products when they found them, but the markings on the crates gave them away. The captain and crew of the Greenpeace vessel were questioned at length by the Russians, but in the end they let them go.."

"Oh, thank God," said Lisa.

"Why do you say that Lisa?" asked Robbie.

"Oh, no particular reason, "replied Lisa. "I am just glad that we now have a clue about what happened to the missing arms."

"Lisa, the big question now is, how did the arms

crates end up on a Greenpeace vessel."

"Yes, I wonder," said Lisa in rather too obviously feigned innocence.

"Lisa, I think you're holding out on us. I think you know something that you're not telling us."

Lisa sighed.

"Well, I guess you might as well know. You already know that I work for the security services in London.

"If those weapons had been delivered to the terrorist organization to which the old Colonel had tried to divert them, they would in all probability have been used in terror attacks on the UK or the US. So they had to be rediverted again away from the terrorist group. I have contacts in Greenpeace and I thought they would be a good home for the weapons."

"You mean you did that, Lisa."

"Yes my job as the Personal Assistant to the Consul General made it quite easy for me. I guess those armaments are now at the bottom of the sea. They can't be used against the Palestinians by the Israelis, and they cant be used against the Israelis, or for that matter against everybody else."

"Good God, Lisa, I had no idea. But why did you not let us now abour your role in all this."

"Roddy, you know as well as I do that this sort of information is only given to others on a strictly 'need to know' basis, and there was no need for you to know. So from your point of view one piece of the puzzle can now be fitted into its place, but there are still a lot of things we don't know and that's why I am working with you all."

"Hold on a moment" said Myra, "I'd like to know

how Rita feels about all this. You work for the Israeli consulate, Rita. Can you still go on working with Lisa knowing what she did?"

"Well, I feel two things," replied Rita. "First, I accept that this information should only be shared on a need to know basis, and I do not feel that my superiors in the consulate need to know. Secondly, I feel that, if the big powers would only stop supplying the Israelis and the Palestinians with arms, the conflict between Israel and Palestine could and would be resolved, so personally I am quite happy that they have been destroyed. And besides, what Lisa did prevented the arms from falling into the hands of Israel's enemies, so as an Israeli I congratulate her. I am very happy to continue working with you all, but I don't think my bosses need to know that I'm doing so."

"Well," said Roddy. "One lives and learns. Why don't we all have a drink to celebrate this new develoment."

Getting kitted Out

Three days after his last visit, Kimpoo returned to see the Colonel. He was accompanied by the same man who had come to take the Colonel's measurements. They carried several boxes.

"Here are your new clothes, Tony. You just have to try everything on. First of all you have to put on a pair of these underpants."

The Colonel did so. Then he tried on shirts. Finally he tried on the navy blue pinstripe suit that they had brought him. He looked at himself in the mirror and was very pleased with what he saw.

"That all looks fine, Kimpoo. What about shoes and socks? I don't see any."

"Don't worry, Tony. They will be coming. All in good time, and besides that I don't think that jacket sits quite right on your shoulders. We'll have it adjusted."

Kimpoo then spoke to the tailor in a language the Colonel did not understand.

"Well, we'll see you again in a few days, Tony."

"Well, for God's sake make it as soon as you can. I can't wait to get out of this place. It's become like a prison."

"Don't worry, Tony, we'll be back soon."

156

Where the trail leads.

After his last meeting with the three angels, Roddy got very busy. With the help of his colleagues and their sources he tried to trace where the Colonel could have been taken. He discussed the issue with Myra.

"It must almost certainly have been a hospital, if they wanted to save his life, and my guess is that it would probably have been one of those fancy hospitals that Brits and Yanks go to for medical procedures that would cost the earth in their own countries."

"Yes, and it would probably have to have been in South East Asia, a hospital not too far from Hangkow."

"Okay, that narrows it down a bit. Let's see, where are there big private hospitals."

"Well, there is the Bumungrad hospital in Bangkok and also the Bangkok Hospital with its branches in other places such as Pattaya and Rayong."

"Yes, and I am sure there must be similar places in Kuala Lumpur, Singapore and Jakarta."

"And I think I heard an item on CNN International about a new super hospital being opened in Brunei. It had been built with money from Saudi Arabia."

"You're right, Myra, and that's just the sort of place he might have been taken too. It is off the beaten path, and that would suit his friends just fine."

"But how can you find out if he is there now?"

"Don't worry, Myra. I have friends in all these places. I am sure they would be able to find out if anyone answering to the Colonel's description was admitted recently with the injuries we know the Colonel had."

"And don't forget his heart problem too."

Roddy got busy on his green phone and made a lot of calls to SIS field offices."

Now he just had to wait for news.

He did not have to wait very long. Less than 48 hours later he received two promising reports. One came from the Supreme Care Hospital in Kuala Lumpur. An elderly man suffering from severe lacerations to his trunk and suffering from a recent heart attack had been admitted there, the day after the events in White and Wong's basement. The second came from the Prince Abdullah hospital in Banda Seri Begawan, the capital of Brunei. This report gave a similar description of the patient and details of his admission, but added that the patient was English speaking and wore a rather large military style moustache.

"I'd put my money on the Brunei hospital," said Myra. It is funded by Arab money whereas I believe the big corporation behind the one in KL is American."

"Okay. There's no time to lose. One of us must fly to Brunei and see if we can confirm that it is the Colonel there. If it isn't, he or she can go on to KL, which is not too far from Brunei, and check there."

"Look, Roddy, I don't think either you or I or Lisa could go because the Colonel would easily recognize us, but I doubt whether he would recognize Rita. Shouldn't we send her."

'Yes, I agree, but I wonder if she would be able to get away. She is after all a Vice Consul at the Israeli consulate.

"Leave it to me, Roddy. I'll have a word with Rita herself first and then I will talk to my Mossad friends. I am sure they could get her released to make a short trip. After all, it is in their interests as well."

So an air ticket and visa were quickly obtained for Rita and off she flew to Brunei. She was a seasoned international traveler and had no difficulty getting a room at the Sheraton and making her way to the hospital. She did not know under what name the Colonel had been admitted, but she did know the date.

She went to the reception desk. "I have come to see that poor man who was admitted last Thursday suffering from those awful injuries and who also had heart problems. I am his niece and we really thought he had had it. We've been so worried."

"Oh, you mean Mr Prendergast. Well, I can tell you that he is recovering very well. He is in room 678 on the sixth floor, and I will gladly take a message to him, but I am afraid he is not being allowed any visitors except for the man who brought him here."

"Oh, dear. I hope I haven't had a wasted journey. I've come all the way from Sydney to see him."

"Well, my dear, I will ask the doctor, but I am afraid the answer will be that he can't have any visitors."

"Oh, well, does he have a phone in his room. If he does, at least I can talk to him on the phone."

" Yes, he does, but I rather think all calls to him have been blocked."

"Well, I'll try anyway. I see there's a phone booth

over there."

Rita walked towards the phone booth, but as soon as she saw that the receptionist was busy with another person, she quickly made for the lifts and went up to the sixth floor. She walked towards room 678. She opened the door very quietly and only slightly so that she could peek in. She did not clearly see the man in pajamas and a dressing gown, who was presumably the patient. He had his back to her, but what she did see was enough to convince her she had come to the right place, for there was another man in the room talking to him, and he had the distinct Asian features of Mr Kimpoo. There was no doubt in Rita's mind that the patient must be the Colonel, but to make doubly sure she wanted to get a glimpse of his features, so she stayed around outside waiting for Kimpoo to leave. She had to wait for thirty minutes. From time to time she had to duck into closets to avoid being seen by Kimpoo or any of the nurses or other staff who might be walking in the corridors, but at last she did manage to get to the Colonel's door, open it just a fraction and look in. There, rather thinner than when she had last seen him, but none the less unmistakeable was the man she had known as Colonel Fairfax.

She hurried back to the hotel and got on the phone immediately to Roddy and informed him, using the code they had agreed on, that the Colonel was indeed in Brunei. She gave him the Colonel's room number in the hospital.

"Did you see anyone else that we know, Rita."

"Yes, I saw Mr Fisher. He was with Uncle Tony when I looked in on him."

"What did they say when they saw you, Rita?

"Nothing Uncle, absolutely nothing. I thought it was very rude of them."

Roddy was pleased; this double speak let him know that she had seen Kimpoo with the Colonel, but that they had not seen her.

"What do you want me to do now Uncle?"

" I would really like to know Mr Fisher's address. Could you find it out for me? There is a parcel I want to send him. I hope that's not too much trouble. What's the weather like out there?"

"It's raining rather a lot."

"But I take it you have your umbrella."

It was true it was the rainy season in Brunei, and Rita prepared herself to follow Kimpoo and find out where he was staying. She had to do this without him ever seeing her.

Rita had to go back to the hospital and hang around for quite some time, without attracting attention to herself, before she saw Kimpoo again. Fortunately it was raining and she was able to use her umbrella not just as protection from the rain, but also as protection from being recognized by Kimpoo. She traced him to an apartment block, but could not follow him inside without arousing his suspicions. There was a doorman at the lobby of the apartment building, She went up to him.

"Excuse me," she said,"but I thought I saw an old friend of mine coming in here, but I wasn't quite sure whether or not it was him. Was it Mr Thomson?"

"No, madam, that was Mr Luk Doo. I don't think we have any Mr Thomson staying here."

"Oh, I'm sorry. I must have made a mistake."

Rita walked quickly back to the Sheraton and made another phone call to Roddy and brought him up to date.

"I'm sorry I could not get his actual apartment number, Uncle," she apologized. "What do I do now?"

"Don't apologize Rita. Congratulations, you have done a terrific job. I think you can come home now."

Roddy immediately got on to his colleagues, using the green phone. He explained the situation.

"I need a sigint team that can bug a couple of rooms in Brunei. Do you have anyone within easy reach of Brunei?"

He went on to describe the two places where he needed the bugs to be placed, the Colonel's hospital room and Kimpoo's apartment, so the team would need to have not only the technical expertise but also the skill to get in unobserved to do the work.

"That's quite an assignment you're talking about," said his colleague. "I'll get back to you as soon as I can."

Myra had been listening to Roddy's phone call.

"What's a sigint team, love?"

"Oh, I thought you as a former Mossad agent would have known that, Myra.

"Sigint means signals intelligence. It used to mean listening in to encrypted messages and then deciphering them, but now we use the expression to mean all kinds of electronic spying."

Roddy got a reply to his call the following day.

"Well, you're in luck, Pi R squared. There's just the team you need in Singapore. They've just completed the job they were doing there and they could be in

Brunei tomorrow."

"By the way, who does the team consist of?"

"It's Nick Sparks and Gordon Wireman. They're a very good team indeed."

"I know," replied Roddy. "I've worked with them before. What names, will they be traveling under?"

"The passports they're currently using are in the names of Frederic Fox and Harold Hare."

"Great. Let them know I'll meet them at the airport in Brunei, if you can just let me know their ETA there."

Brunei

Lisa had a very busy time the next day, getting the air booking to Brunei for Roddy, and getting rooms reserved at the serviced apartments where Kimpoo was staying. She was lucky; there were two apartments vacant.

So Roddy flew off to Brunei the next day and landed at the airport just over an hour before the flight carrying the sigint team was due to arrive. They all piled into a taxi and made off to the apartment building.

The two members of the sigint team presented a remarkable contrast in style and in appearance. Nick Sparks had a miserable looking face. He was in his mid fifties and had a north country accent. He was in fact a semi-retired cat burglar, and a very good one. It took many years before the CID in Britain were able to catch him out, but then the SIS had stepped in and made him an offer that it would have been difficult for him to refuse, as the alternative was a very long prison sentence. So he was employed to work with electronic surveillance experts. His main task was to get into places that SIS wanted bugged and to enable his colleague to get in as well without either of them being detected. He had also

164

developed a good deal of expertise in the use of the electronic equipment used by his colleagues, so he made an excellent partner for what he called the spy nerds.

Gordon Wireman was half Sparks's age. He came from Somerset and had a faintly country accent. He had curly blond hair and bright blue eyes, which always seemed to be smiling. Many men thought he must be gay, and many women found him adorable. The fact that he was not in fact gay could be deduced from the string of girl friends he had all over the world, in just about every country where he had ever worked. But none of them ever suspected what his real work was. He enjoyed working with Nick and they complemented each other extremely well.

After they had checked in and unpacked their rather unusual suitcases, which had been specially designed by Wireman to fool airport X-ray machines into thinking that the suitcases contained only normal clothing and personal stuff, they needed to find out which apartment Kimpoo occupied. They accomplished this quite easily. Wireman went to the receptionist's desk and started talking to her. He asked her about things to do and see in Bandar Siri Begawan, eventually getting her to come outside so that she would point out the directions to get to the city's attractions. Then Nick moved out of the shadows and behind her desk. He looked through the register to discover which apartment was occupied by Mr Luk Doo. It was apartment D on the third floor. He then went back upstairs to the apartment he was sharing with Nick.

Nick meanwhile spent another fifteen minutes or

so flirting with the receptionist, who, he discovered, was from the Philippines. She was happy to spend time talking to this good looking and very attentive new guest in the apartment house. He on the other hand had gathered a great deal of information about the other people staying there and was particularly interested to hear about the Arab visitors who frequently came to see Mr Luk Doo.

The next problem was how to get into Kimpoo's apartment. Picking the lock on his door would present no problem to Nick, but it could only be done when Kimpoo was out.

Their luck was with them once again. It had been agreed that when Kimpoo went out, Roddy would follow him. Roddy was pleased to find that Kimpoo headed for the hospital. On his green phone he kept the sigint team informed of his movements. They had told him that they only needed about twenty minutes to get into the flat and install all their bugging devices. It took ten minutes to walk to the hospital. Roddy phoned to tell the team that he thought it OK for them to go in and install the equipment. Meanwhile he hung around the hospital lobby, looking at the bookshop there, and having a very leisurely cup of coffee at the Dunkin Donuts.

Kimpoo eventually came down into the lobby on his way out about half an hour later. Roddy let the team know that he was on his way back. "You've got about ten minutes to finish up," he told them.

"Don't worry. We're just packing up now," replied Wireman.

"Okay. Now we've got to bug the Colonel's room in the hospital."

"That should be easy enough," said Sparks. "It's on the 6th floor, so I won't try to get in from the outside. We'll just put on overalls and go in to adjust the Colonel's television."

"Just like that?'

"Yes. I found that early on in my previous career," Sparks laughed. "When they see men in overalls with a tool belt around them and a clip board, people always assume that they are on legitimate business. I'm sure it will work here just as well as it does in London."

He proved to be right. The two men walked in to the hospital, took the lift up to the sixth floor and to the Colonel's room. They went in.

"Mr Pendergast, is it, sir"

"Yes, I'm Prendergast," replied the Colonel

"We've come to fix your television, sir."

"I didn't know there was anything wrong with it."

"Well, we'll just look at it, sir."

The two men proceeded to take the TV apart and put it together again. Wireman had actually put some new parts into the set, as well as planting the bugs inside it. So when the set was turned on again, the picture genuinely was clearer than it had been.

"There you are, Sir. I think you'll find that's better."

"Yes, you're right it is much clearer now. Thank you very much."

"It's all part of the service, Sir," said Sparks and off they went.

Back at the apartments they set up the receiving equipment for both sources, Kimpoo's house and the Colonel's room. The equipment included recording devices.

"Now comes the dead boring part," Wireman said to Roddy, "waiting for the information you want to come across."

In fact it turned out not to take as long as they had feared. Kimpoo came back to see the Colonel the next day and they heard him tell the Colonel to be ready to move,.

"I will bring you your shoes and outerwear. "We have ordered a bullet proof vest for you, as it turns out that there are a number of British and Israeli agents around who might want to take a shot at you. We don't want you killed as we have a very important job for you to do. I know the bullet proof vest will seem a bit heavy and inconvenient, but you'll be safer with it on. And we will give you a lightweight coat to wear over it."

"Where are you going to take me, Kimpoo?"

"Well, Tony I can't tell that yet, but I can tell you it will involve a short flight."

Roddy conveyed all this back to the three Angels in Hangkow. He then discussed with the sigint team what to do next.

"I think two of us should be concentrating on what we get from the bugs in the hospital and from those in Kimpoo's apartment. But I also think one of us had better follow Kimpoo when he goes out. I know he's up to something but I am not sure what."

"Well, you're the one who is probably best trained to shadow him" said Sparks. "Why don't you take on that, and we'll stay here monitoring the bugs."

This was agreed and next morning Roddy made his way dressed in the typical dark blue shirt and trousers of a peasant farmer and hung about outside the apartment block where Kimpoo was staying, without making himself at all conspicuous.

About ten o'clock Kimpoo came out of the building and went first to a big department store. He came out carrying two identical suitcases. They were relatively small ones with wheels, and could be used on an airline as hand baggage. He went back to his apartment with these. Half an hour later he came out again and this time he headed for a travel agency. Using a gadget that Nick Sparks had given him Roddy was able to stand a little way away from the entrance to the travel agents and listen in to the conversation there. He heard Kimpoo book two business class tickets on a flight to Jakarta leaving in two days time.

After that Kimpoo got into a taxi and went off. Roddy tried to take another taxi, but when the driver saw the grubby looking peasant that Roddy appeared to be, he refused to take him and he lost Kimpoo.

So he went back to the apartment block where Kimpoo stayed and waited there until he returned. Roddy observed a number of people coming and going from the apartment building but there was no way he could tell whether any of them had been coming from or going to Kimpoo's apartment. Eventually he went back to join the two men in the sigint team and after telling them what he had found out he got on the green phone again to relay the information to the Angels.

"I want one of you to get to Jakarta by the next available flight" he said. "Book yourself into a hotel in the center of the town and wait there for instructions. "

"I think it might be best if you were the one to go there, Rita, and find out where you can find a motor bike to rent in a hurry in case we need it. Do you know your way around Jakarta at all?"

"Yes, Roddy, I once spent three weeks there when I was with a traveling stunt show."

"That's great, Rita. It may turn out that you will need your knowledge of the ciry."

The next day the eavesdroppers heard Kimpoo arrive at the Colonel's room at the hospital. Roddy had followed him there from his apartment but nothing of interest had occurred.

"Good morning, Tony," said Kimpoo's cheerful voice. "Your time here is going to come to an end tomorrow. I have brought you a new passport. It's British and it's in the name of Major Desmond Astor. I have also booked you into one of the best five star hotels in Jakarta. It's the PanAsia Grand. I am sure you'll love it there. "

"When do I get my shoes? I can't bloody well travel barefoot."

"You'll get those tomorrow. They're special hand-made shoes and they're not quite ready yet, but they will be tomorrow, I promise. And I'll also bring the special vest to protect you plus the light jacket to wear over it."

"Won't they be a bit suspicious when I go through airport security with all that clobber on? They'll probably make me take it all off and they'll put it through the X Ray machine."

"Oh," said Kimpoo airily. "We'll cross that bridge when we come to it. It will all go smoothly I tell you."

The Big Bang Theory

With the help of the sigint team Roddy was able to arrange a secure international conference call to the three angels. He passed on all the information that he and the sigint team had gathered.

"I have a very ominous feeling," he told them, "I have a strong feeling that something very important, something possibly disastrous, is about to happen."

"Yes," agreed Myra, "I never thought that Kimpoo had much of a sense of humor."

"What do you mean?"

"Didn't anything strike you about the new name they have given the Colonel, the name on his new passport."

"You mean Major Desmond Astor?"

"Yes."

"What about it?"

"Well, the short form of Desmond is Des. So what does that make his name? What does it sound like?"

"Oh, my God, Major Des Astor.

"Exactly. They've called him 'major disaster.' I'm surprised the Colonel hasn't tumbled to it."

"I suspect that all the time the Colonel has been in

the hospital, they've been keeping him mildly sedated. Just enough for it to cloud his thinking processes."

"And that's not the only thing that is suspicious. You know who owns the PanAsia hotel chain? It's a very big Israeli corporation, and a major UN conference on counter terrorism is scheduled to start there tomorrow. I don't suppose the Colonel knows anything about this, but I don't believe it is just coincidence that he has been booked in there."

"But what could they achieve by just having the Colonel staying there?"

"I'm not sure. I don't think they trust the Colonel, but they did talk about his next assignment without giving him any idea what it was to be."

"Yes, and maybe having him in the hotel could help them gain access to something or somebody,"

"Maybe, but in that case why don't they let him know? Why are they keeping the old bugger in the dark?" He then addressed Rita in Jakarta. "Rita, are you settled in all right?"

"Sure. I'm staying at the Hilton which is about a mile away from the PanAsia Grand."

"Could you get there in a hurry, if it was necessary?"

"Well, I have a good bike standing ready for when I need it, but the traffic here can be horrendous, especially at rush hour and rush hour seems to last virtually all day."

"Well, unless someone has any bright ideas I think we had all better sleep on what we know and I'll call you all again in about ten hours time, but please stay near a phone in case anything turns up."

Roddy and the sigint team continued their round-the-clock monitoring of the Colonel's hospital room and Kimpoo's apartment.

When it was about 9 a.m. local time the next morning Nick Sparks who was listening in on Kimpoo's apartment heard movement from there and conversation between two men. It was in Bahasa Indonesia, the local language and fortunately Sparks had some knowledge of that tongue. As far as he could gather the new voice was saying something about having brought the equipment. He also heard him ask a question about the other suitcase. He reported this immediately to Roddy. But just at that moment his phone rang. It was Lisa and from her tone of voice he gathered that what she had to say was urgent.

"Roddy, Myra and I think we have solved the mystery. We think the Colonel is being used as a human bomb and that they're using him to get into the hotel with his suitcase which will turn out to be a bomb. The so called bulletproof vest is probably nothing of the kind and it too is probably packed with explosives. And maybe his special handmade shoes are bombs too. I think you've got to warn the people there immediately. The Colonel probably doesn't have a clue what's going on. He's become expendable so they're just using him."

"Excuse me, sir," interupted Nick Sparks. "I think you ought to know that Kimpoo is just leaving his apartment to take the Colonel to the airport."

The Happy Traveller on the Road to Glory

The Colonel was quite happy to see Kimpoo the next day. Kimpoo handed him his new shoes.

"Try them, on, Tony – or rather I should be calling you Des now, shouldn't I? That's the name on your new passport, and your must admit it is quite a passport. Have you looked at it carefully?"

"Yes, and I admit I was surprised to see you had got me a British Diplomatic passport. How the hell did you manage that?

"We have our resources, Des, and we thought it would help you in getting through security and immigration.. The immigration officers will be expecting a lot of UN and diplomatic people coming to Jakarta today."

"Oh, why's that?"

"I thought you would have heard about that from the news on the TV, but I guess you have not been listening to the international news channels. The fact is there is a big UN conference in the hotel where you'll be staying. You'll be able to mix with all sorts of VIPs, but I should stay away from the Brits if I were you. They might wonder who you are."

The Colonel tried on his new shoes. They seemed

quite comfortable.

"Got your suitcase packed, Des?" asked Kimpoo.

"Yes."

"OK, then let's go. We'll get to the airport in good time. Here let me help you on with your bullet proof vest and this light coat to go over it."

"Won't I look rather too warmly dressed for this climate?"

"Maybe, but you can't go around obviously wearing a bulletproof vest, can you? And anyway you're a Brit and we Asians expect British people to be somewhat eccentric."

The Colonel put on the vest and the coat and they set out for the car. On the way out of the hospital, Kimpoo told him. "All the medical bills for Mr Prendergast have been paid, so we can just walk out now."

There was a car waiting for them just outside the main entrance to the hospital. Kimpoo put their suitcases in the trunk and then got in beside the driver. The Colonel sat in the back seat. At the back of his mind the Colonel had the feeling that something wasn't quite right, but he was not sure what it was.

He asked Kimpoo. "What exactly is it that you want me to do in Jakarta, Kimpoo?"

"Well, Des, I don't exactly know myself. All I can tell you is that when you check in at reception in the hotel you will receive a message that will make everything clear to you."

At the airport the Colonel went through security with no trouble. Kimpoo spoke briefly to the security people at the X-Ray machines and the Colonel and his baggage were passed through without him having to take off his coat and shoes, as other passengers had to. He assumed that this was due to his having a diplomatic passport, but he did think he saw Kimpoo passing some money to the agent at the machine.

The relatively short flight to Jakarta passed pleasantly enough. Kimpoo sat beside him reading a James Bond spy novel. There was little or no conversation between them. When their flight landed at Soekarno-Hatta Airport in Jakarta the Colonel again went through cusstoms and immigration with no difficulty.

Outside the airport building there was a car to meet them. Kimpoo took the Colonel's suitcase and put it in the trunk of the car together with his own identical case. They drove off. The drive from the airport to the PanAsia Grand Hotel took over an hour. Kimpoo was rather quiet during the drive not like his usually rather flamboyant and talkative self. As they approached the area in which the hotel was situated he saw that the streets seemed very deserted.

"It's unusually quiet today," he said to the Colonel "usually this place is teeming with people. I wonder if people are being kept away from here because of the UN conference."

"Well, I hope I won't have any trouble checking into the hotel."

"Don't worry, Des, I'm sure everything will be all right."

Finally they were at the hotel. Kimpoo got out and handed the Colonel his suitcase.

"This is where we say Goodbye" he said. I will be off now. You just go in and register at reception." He got back in the car and drove off.

The Colonel was surprised at this abrupt departure. Kimpoo had always stuck to him like glue every step of the way, but now he seemed to be in a great hurry to be off. To add to his surprise he found that no porter came to take his bag. This was supposed to be a five star hotel. He looked at the suitcase. He had tied a name tag on to his suitcase and this one had no name tag on it. Slowly the penny dropped and he realized that the suitcase was almost certainly a bomb. His bullet proof vest was probably a bomb too. He was a living, walking terrorist bomb. He threw the suitcase into the lobby of the hotel, to get it as far away from himself as he could. Then he started to rip off the light weight coat he had on and get rid of the 'bullet proof vest', but Kimpoo had made a very thorough job of fastening it to him when he put it on. He struggled to undo all the fasteners.. He knew he had no time to lose.

Kimpoo had not got very far away in the car. He opened the glove compartment and took out a small electronic device. He too knew he had no time to lose. Somewhere something had gone wrong.

The Big Bang

Meanwhile back in Brunei, Roddy was very busy on his green phone. He called his opposite number in the British Embassy in Jakarta,

"Hello, 2 Pi R, this is Pi R squared calling from Brunei. We have every reason to believe that a terrorist bomb attack is about to be made very shortly on the PanAsia Grand hotel in Jakarta. I want you to warn the Ambassador and get him to warn the Indonesian authorities. There is hardly any time to waste as this is all going to happen within two or three hours."

"Can you give me any more details?'

"We are virtually certain that the bomb will be in the luggage of an elderly Briton traveling under the name of Major Desmond Astor and carrying a forged British diplomatic passport. As far as we know he does not know that he is in fact an unwitting suicide bomber. He may well be accompanied by a much younger Oriental looking man who is of mixed Hambonian and Palestinian parentage. The name we have for him is Kimpoo, but of course we do not know whether that is his real name or an alias. But please hurry: they may have to evacuate the area around the hotel to avoid casualties.."

"Okay, I'll get on to His Excellency right away but he may take a bit of convincing and then he has to convince the Indonesian authorities that the threat is real. Do you think the Indonesian intelligence people have any idea of what's going on?"

"I very much doubt it, but it would not be a bad idea for you to contact them and pass on this info."

"Will do. I'll contact you later."

Meanwhile Lisa had got on the phone to the Hilton and asked to be put through to Rita's room.

"I am sorry, madam, but there's no answer from her room phone."

"Then please, please, page her. This is a matter of life and death."

"Very well, madam, if you say so."

Lisa waited till the phone went dead.

"What do we do now", she asked Myra.

"We keep trying" said Myra. "You keep on bugging the hotel operator and meanwhile I think I have Rita's cell phone number somewhere. I don't know whether an international call I make from my cell phone will get through to her, but I'll try."

It took nearly an hour until they finally managed to get through to Rita.

Roddy, himself spoke to her from Brunei,

"Rita, can you go as quickly as you can to the PanAsia Grand hotel. Tell the hotel receptionist and the manager if you can get hold of him that there is a serious threat that an attempt will shortly be made to blow up the hotel and everybody in it, including all those VIP guests there for the UN conference. You may have some difficulty persuading them, but it is vital that they evacuate the hotel and its immediate surrounding."

"Okay, Roddy, but the traffic is very heavy and it may not be easy to get there quickly"

"I trust you, Rita. I know you're a great stunt rider. If you can't get there quickly no one can."

"All right, Roddy, I'm off."

She went to collect the bike she had arranged for, and drove hell for leather to the hotel. She squeezed around cars, buses and other motor bikes. She drove on whichever side of the road she could get through quicker and frequently she rode on the sidewalk. She heard cops blowing their whistles and shouting but she took no notice She found she had two police motor-cycle cops on her tail but they were no match for her stunt driving skills. She got to the hotel and rode her bike up the steps into the lobby on her bike. She told a startled receptionist. "I must speak to the manager."

The receptionist had no desire to argue with this apparently crazy woman, and she called the manager immediately.

As the manager approached Rita shouted at him. "There's going to be a terrorist bomb attack on the hotel any minute now. You've got to evacuate everyone out of the hotel and as far away from it as they can get and you've got to do it immediately."

The manager said "I have no idea who you are Miss. But I have no intention of scaring all my guests because of some unconfirmed story from a total stranger."

"Then you'll be responsible for many deaths,

including your own."

"Please leave quietly, Miss, or I will have to call security."

Rita's response was to reach across the receptionist's desk and pick up a telephone. The surprised manager hardly realized what was happening. Rita brought the phone down hard on his head, leaving him dazed and him almost unconscious.

She turned to the terrified looking receptionist, "Where's the hotel's public address system?"

The receptionist pointed.

"How does it work? I need to get a message to everyone in the hotel."

The receptionist explained the system.

Rita began speaking loudly into the phone the receptionist had handed her.

"Attention all guests and staff, this is an extremely urgent message. All guests and all staff must immediately vacate the hotel as there is a very serious threat of a bomb attack on the hotel."

She repeated the message twice more. Then she handed the phone back to the receptionist and told her to keep repeating the same message over and over again until people started streaming out of the hotel. She then started running around the hotel knocking on doors and telling everyone she came across to get out of the hotel immediately.

Some of the delegates to the United Nations conference tried to argue with her, but she simply replied to them, "All right stay here and be killed if you are so keen to die."

By the time Rita felt reasonably certain that the

hotel was being steadily vacated by all the staff and guests, she went to the receptionist who was still giving out the warning message.

"Come with me."

She got to her motorbike and told the receptionist to ride on the pillion seat behind her and she roared off. She went about five hundred yards away from the hotel but as the road was straight she could still see the hotel. "I think we should be safe here." She dismounted and the shaking receptionist did so too. She was glad to see that there seemed to be no traffic on the roads near the hotel.

Then she saw a single car drive up outside the hotel.

....

Meanwhile the SIS agent attached to the Embassy had managed to convince the Ambassador of the need for immediate action and the Ambassador in turn had after a rather long conversation managed to contact the Indonesian Minister of Internal Affairs, who had then ordered the Chief of Police to close all the roads within a half kilometer radius of the hotels and to evacuate everyone in the same area.

Roddy's colleague 2 PI R phoned Roddy to tell him what had been achieved. But while he was speaking on the phone Roddy heard a very loud noise come over the phone line.

....

Kimpoo had realized that the Indonesians must have got hold of information about the coming bombing. He realized that he had to act immediately. He pressed a button on the electronic device he had taken from the glove drawer of the car.

The Colonel, standing just outside the hotel, was still struggling to get out of his bullet proof vest. He never succeeded.

The bombs went off demolishing most of the hotel and some of the surrounding property including the car in which Kimpoo was travelling. The bombs were, as Myra and the others had suspected, in the suitcase and in the "bullet proof vest", though not in the shoes, which were a pair of genuine hand made shoes. It seemed a pity that such a nice new pair of shoes had to be destroyed.

Thanks to the quick actions taken by Roddy and his colleagues at one level and by Rita on another, there were no casualties except for the Colonel, Kimpoo and the driver of the car. The property damage however was in the millions of dollars.

Aftermath

There were enormous differences in the way in which these events were reported in the newspapers in different countries. Some of the Arabic papers, especially those published in Palestine referred to the late Colonel as a senior British army officer who had gallantly fought for the Palestinian cause and had given his life for it. Of course those Arabs who had actually known the Colonel knew that this was absolute B.S. They knew him as a traitorous scoundrel who could not be trusted an inch, but who had proved useful for a while in the Palestinian struggle against Israel. The Daily Mirror in London's headline screamed "Disgraced ex-Sergeant Major becomes first Western suicide bomber." The New York Times got most of the facts wrong and wrote "Another British Secret Agent turns traitor" and in reasonably polite language went on to imply that this was what one might expect from the intelligence services of those wretched Limeys.

The broadcast and cable networks all had fun with the news with their different takes. Bill O'Reilly suggested that the United States should break off all diplomatic ties with the United Kingdom and subject the country to the harshest sanctions. The so-called English muffin should be renamed the Republican Toastie. This caused some amusement among Brits since, to the best of their knowledge, the "English" muffin was an American invention anyway. Jay Leno got back at Bill O'Reilly by suggesting it be called the Democratic Bun. However to this day it is still known as the English muffin.

Did anything good come out of the whole affair? One of the sources of the flow of arms to the middle East was blocked. Russia refused to supply any more arms to the Israelis. The Israelis had refused to pay for the arms shipment that first the Colonel and then later Lisa had diverted and were now probably at the bottom of the sea, but the Russians insisted that they should receive full payment as they had shipped the arms. So in the end the whole contract was cancelled.

Questions were asked in the parliaments of a number of countries including the U.S. Congress. Had the CIA known what was going on? And if so, what action had been taken to prevent the loss of property that had resulted from the bombing in Jakarta? Answer: none, though a rather feeble attempt was made to claim credit for the warnings that resulted in the evacuation of the whole area around the hotel so that no loss of life, other than the lives of the perpetrators, had occurred. However this story did not wash as it soon became quite clear that it was the work of the British SIS and an Israeli Vice Consul from Hambonia who had given the warnings. (No one however was able to explain why an Israeili Vice Consul in Hambonia just happened to be in Djakarta in time to give those warnings.) The fact was that the CIA had decided that Hambonia had no oil and was a little country of no importance and their local agents had been totally unaware of anything that was going on there. In reality, of course, the country was the location of a great deal of overt and covert intelligence gathering by the other major powers.

The Israeli government took all the credit it could for the unauthorized activities of its junior Vice Consul in Hambonia, which it stressed had saved thousands of lives. They, however, made no mention of the Palestinian lives that had been spared by the blockage of the Russian arms supplies.

The Hambonians tried to take credit for whatever it could, but no body ever listened to what the Hambonians had to say anyway

As for the people concerned in these events, the authorities in Britain, in Israel, and in Hambonia all agreed not to take any action against Lady Ponsonby for her rather ambiguous role in the events. She was not however given any more assignments by Mossad, and many uncertainties still remained about whose side, if any, she had really been on.

Jack MacKay, alias Roddy O'Bhuzaigh, alias, Sid Bloggs, alias Pi R squared, went on eventually to become the head of the SIS and became Sir Jack. He also became known within the service as Fibonacci, or Fibber, or sometimes 235813213455 when he was referred to in coded transmissions, though any other group of numbers in the Fibonacci series would do equally well.

When he got back to Hangkow after all the problems arising from the Colonel's explosive death had been cleared up, there was still one bit of the whole mystery that puzzled him.

Why on earth had the British Ambassador to Hambonia recomended to the Foreign Office that the Colonel should become the Acting Consul General. It went against all the normal rules and from the start it had seemed to all the members of the Consulate staff a most unsuitale appointment.

The Consul would have been quite capable of taking over the CG's post either in an acting or substantive capacity. So why had the Colonel been appointed?

He decided he wanted to get to the bottom of this, so he consulted his colleagues in the the capital, Pispot. Through their contacts they discovered the answer. It turned out that while his wife had been away on a visit to her aging parents in Scotland, the Ambassador had taken advantage of the opportunities offered by the less respectable offerings of the "entertainment" sector of the place and had done so rather indiscreetly.

He had actually been caught on videotape frolicking in an upstairs room of a rather notorious go-go bar with two young Hambonian women. In the video neither the two girls nor the ambassador himself had a stitch of clothing on and the activities they were engaged in were far from the kind of activities normally discussed at meetings of the Hangkow International Ladies club. The Sissies actually managed to obtain one copy of the videotape and passed it on upwards. It was the copy that had been sent to the Ambassador and with which he had been blackmailed into doing what the organization behind the Colonel told him to do.

The Foreign Office recalled the Ambassador and he was given early retirement. The tape circulated rather freely among some of the senior members at the F.O. and were even used in training sessions for young diplomats, as a warning about the kind of behavior to avoid (or at least being caught doing it.)

When Jack was knighted, Myra, as his wife, became Lady MacKay. This made Lady Ponsonby absolutely furious. How could Myra think she was her equal, so she decided to do something about it. She discovered that the Earl of Haringey had not remarried after divorcing his wife, so she set her cap at him and they were later married in St. George's, Hanover Square. Thus Lady P became the Countess of Haringey, and she could still consider herself superior to Myra.

Myra could not have cared less. She decided to go back to the London School of Economics and obtain a Ph.D. She then went on to teach at the University of Edinburgh, eventually becoming Professor and Chair of the Economics Department. Her book on the Economics of Warfare became a classic and won her a Nobel prize. King Charles decided to make her a Dame (equivalent to a knight) so she now had a title in her own right, not simply a courtesy title given to her because of her husband's rank, and she became Dame Myra MacKay.

It was rumored that someone, possibly Rita Riker, had pointed out to the Countess of Haringey that Dame Myra had earned a title by her work and not by sleeping with a titled man. The former Lady Ponsonby was not amused.

Kimpoo had no close relatives and he was quickly

and completely forgotten by all those involved.

The Canadian secret service decided to pension off Messrs White and Wong, but they were happy enough to continue to practice law in Hangkow. The basement where the Colonel had been interrogated was turned into a wine cellar, and you can now get some of the world's finest wines there.

Lisa was brought back to London by her employers at MI5. She received a promotion for the work she had done in Hambonia, and shortly after Jack Mackay had become head of the SIS she was made head of MI5. There followed a period of unusually close cooperation between the two services. Like Myra she was eventually made a Dame as well.

Rita decided to leave the Israeli diplomatic service and to return to the circus. The life there had been so much more exciting than the work of an Israeli Vice Consul had been, except for that exciting period when she had been one of the three Roddy's Angels. She was also finding it more and more difficult to justify Israel's actions in Gaza. So she returned to Britain and joined Hammerfields Circus. She still did motorcycle stunts but gradually she began to take on a more managerial role. In due course she took over the circus and re-named it Ryker's Circus and Stunt Show. She expanded and created branches in South Africa, in Australia, and in Rome. Ryker's Circus is now a global business, and the shows all travel, so you may find a branch of Ryker's Circus coming your way any time, though probably Rita herself will not be performing.

The Mackays, Dame Lisa, and the impresario Rita Ryker have remained close friends throughout the years, and have a special get together once a year on the anniversary of the Colonel's death and they drink an ironic toast to him as the man who brought them all to-gether.

More from
Four Pillars Media Group

If you enjoyed **The Spyder's Web,** watch out for
Eavesdropping on Adolf Hitler
Ian Mayo-Smith**'s** true account of his work in World War II
as a code breaker at the world famous Bletchley Park crypto-
graphy center, coming shortly from FPMG.

Other books by Ian available from FPMG include
PEACE - Poems, Essays And Comments for Everyone
and
Trying to Walk the Way
Both these books are collections of Ian's poetry and essays
on contemporary issues.

The Children's Aviary
a little book about some rather unusual birds, such as the
Messy Nester Hawk, the YakYak, and the Humphus Pumphus
delightully illustrated by Andrea Doty. For children of all ages.

Positive People
co-written with Catherine Wyatt-Morley.

Catherine was a faithful wife and mother of three
childen, when she learnt that her unfaithful husband had
infected her with the HIV virus. She lost her job and even
her priest turned against her but she is a woman with an
indomitable spirit. She went on to found a major organization
offering education and help to others infected with or affected
by this dread disease. You may have heard Catherine on
national television, but watch out for her latest book
My Life with AIDS: From Tragedy to Triumph
coming soon from FPMG.

Imagine a child-molesting Catholic priest becoming the Pope. What would you do if you had been one of that monster's innocent victims? Read how victim Ben Clancy deals with the situation in the dramatic thriller,

The Crumbling Empire

by Brian Walsh and Maura Satchell. Already available as an e-book for the Nook or Kindle, as well as in print.

Watch out too for the sequel
The Song of Revolution

All these books can be obtained direct from the publisher,
Four Pillars Media Group,
P. O. Box 499, Meriden, CT 06450.